KU-150-917

MOONE BOY

THE NOTION POTION

Also available

Moone Boy: The Blunder Years

Moone Boy: The Fish Detective

Moone Boy: The Marvellous Activity Manual

Chris O'Dowd & Nick V. Murphy

MOONE BOY

THE NOTION POTION

ILLUSTRATED BY

WALTER GIAMPAGLIA/CARTOON SALOON

MACMILLAN CHILDREN'S BOOKS

First published 2017 by Macmillan Children's Books
an imprint of Pan Macmillan
20 New Wharf Road, London N1 9RR
Associated companies throughout the world
www.panmacmillan.com

ISBN 978-1-5098-1352-0

With thanks to Sky, Baby Cow Productions and Sprout Pictures

1 3 5 7 9 8 6 4 2

A CIP catalogue record for this book is available from the British Library.

Printed and bound by CPI Group (UK) Ltd, Croydon CR0 4YY

To Dawn,

holder of hands, maker of love,

mother of dragons.

Chris

For Vicki, my favourite Realsie,

who's such a perfect partner-

in-crime, I often wonder if she's

really an IW (Imaginary Wife).

Nick

WELCOME TO THE BOOK!

I was born under a wandering star. A wandering, wandering star. It was completely lost, in fact. The mistake the star made was getting peckish as it neared the Milky Way. Starved and confused, the sky-strolling star tried to take a bite out of the chocolatey-sounding galaxy before being chased off.

Of course, I, Sean 'Caution!' Murphy, am not alone in this detail. All imaginary friends (IFs) are born under wandering stars. It's kinda our 'thing'. Apart from Dicky 'Single Tooth' Magnusson, who was famously born under a cartwheeling comet. This common place of birth gives all IFs a keen sense of adventure, a passion for science, non-science and nonsense, and the sensation of always feeling slightly lost.

The reason I bring up my birth is that our story begins on the magical morning of my birthday. Now, usually I'm not one to hoot too loudly about getting older, but this year was different. By anybody's standards, I'd had a pretty terrific twelve months. A year earlier, I'd been a lowly clerk in the customer services department of C.L.I.F.F. – the Corporate League of Imaginary Friends Federation. But then a twist of fate had brought me to the attention of an idiot boy from the west of Ireland.

Together with Martin Moone, I'd had quite the year of adventure. We'd found a new home for a misplaced loony IF, Loopy Loopington Lou. We'd thwarted a mysterious plot in a local fish factory, and hosted Christmas for some Brazilian fish-gutters. Martin had even been bitten by a mole, which we'd thought was radioactive and had given us superpowers, but instead this turned out to be rabies. Yes, quite the year! And given that I'd behaved wonderfully as an imaginary companion throughout, I was expecting my birthday present to be nothing short of spectacular.

If I'm honest, being an IF can sometimes be a thankless job. You're a constant Giver, listening to your Realsie's gripes and grumbles. Give advice, give encouragement, give high-fives – give, give, give. At different times you assume the role of Best Bud, Confidant or sometimes even Parent (but without the weekly joy of receiving six gold coins from the government. You do know that the government gives your parents six gold coins every week, right? Of course you do. I mean, why else would your mam and dad do it?!).

However, an IF's birthday is the one time when the Giver becomes the Getter. A Realsie can surprise their IF with almost any kind of gift *imaginable*! Think about that. ANYTHING!

Now, I'm no fool, so I understood that Martin was often lacking in the imagination department. Yet my hopes were high. If there's one thing I've learned since I was born under a wandering star it's that sometimes the universe can surprise you. Or chase you.

And so, on the eve of my birthday, I kept my fingers crossed, my toes clenched and my tongue in my ear. That's how I always make wishes – and it's also how I tell stories. So please enjoy this story about what actually happened on my birthday, and the mysteries, magic and mayhem that followed. Relish the words. Read it aloud in the voice of someone you think sounds ridiculous. As you turn the pages, feed grapes to a nearby goldfish. Or just sit and read it like normal.

Signed,

Sean

Sean

P.S. Only feed grapes to your goldfish if his name is Goldington 'Grapenuts' McFinns. He's the only one I know who actually likes them.

CHAPTER ONE
BREAKFAST OF CHAMPIONS

On the morning of the big day, when the sun finally peeked through the filthy windows of Martin Moone's bedroom, I'd already been awake for three hours. I was the kind of giddy you only get a few times a year: Christmas morning, obviously; then Swan Night (that magical hour at dusk on 24th September when swans break their silence and speak perfect English); and, of course, your birthday! I WAS GIDDY AS A GIGGLING GOAT! I'd been absent-mindedly whistling for about twenty minutes by the time the Moone boy slowly prised open his dopey eyes to find me pacing at the end of his bed.

'GOOD MORNING, MARTIN!' I squealed casually.

'Oh my goodness,' he croaked. 'Good morning, Sean.'

'Hope I didn't wake you.'

I whistled some more. Martin could obviously sense my excitement, and sat up.

'I see it's that special time again, Sean!'

'Are you referring to your class science trip?'

'No, Sean. I hadn't forgotten that, but I think we both know there's something *even more* special today, don't we?'

'Well, yes, I suppose we do, my good friend,' I replied sheepishly, trying to pretend that my birthday had slipped my mind.

'It feels like it comes around quicker every time!'

'Yup. As they say, Martin, time flies like an arrow; fruit flies like a banana.'

'Who says that?'

'One of the Marx brothers – Karl, I believe.'

'Well, Sean, I can't lie – I've been looking forward to this ever since I woke up nearly two minutes ago. It's my very favourite time.

I wonder what we have in store today?'

'Haha, yes. What do you think is planned, Martin?'

'Well, I don't know, but I suppose we'll both find out when we get to the kitchen.'

'The . . . kitchen?' I asked, beginning to lose confidence.

'Of course. Where else would we have *breakfast time*?!'

With that, Martin skipped off down the hall, his big, lazy noggin knocking door frames and dashing my hopes as he went.

I trudged after him, disappointed but not massively surprised, and could hear the wee eejit yelping from the kitchen, 'Woo-hoo! READYBIX! Yes!'

(I should probably point out that he has the same breakfast every single morning.)

Martin guzzled down his brown, stodgy boy-fuel as his three sisters woke from their slumbers and joined him at the breakfast table. He'd made a checklist for the school science trip and was marking off items between mouthfuls.

Checklist

- Shoes. ☑
- Spare shoes in case of science fire. ☑
- Colouring pencils. ☑
- Some cheese. ☐
- Stolen Walkman from Trisha's room. ☐
- Cushion for springy bus seat. ☐
- Francie Feeley's finest sherbet. ☑
- Lucky rabbit's fist. ☐
- Checklist. ☐

'Martin, what's the flippin' point of putting "checklist" on your checklist?' barked Sinead, the youngest and fiercest of his three older sisters.

'Well, it's to make sure I do a checklist, dummy.'

'But you've obviously already done it if there's a list to put it on,' chimed in their eldest sister, Fidelma.

'Exactly!' Martin said, tapping his nose as if his plan was faultless.

'Let him do his silly list,' Trisha, the moody middle sister, sniggered. 'I bet he won't even manage to check off the fact he has a checklist, the tool.'

Martin quickly checked the box next to 'Checklist', hoping nobody would notice. Seeing this, his sisters burst out laughing.

The fearsome threesome were being particularly vicious lately. I guessed they were feeling rather superior, basking in the success of recent triumphs. Fidelma had just done very well in her Mock Leaving Cert* and was studying

***MOCK LEAVING CERT** – a trial exam carried out by students about to do their final school exams. If they do badly, they are severely ridiculed by teachers, parents and pets. Or mocked.

hard for the proper exams.

Trisha had recently won a student design award for a nose ring, inspired by a book she'd found on Spanish bullfighting.

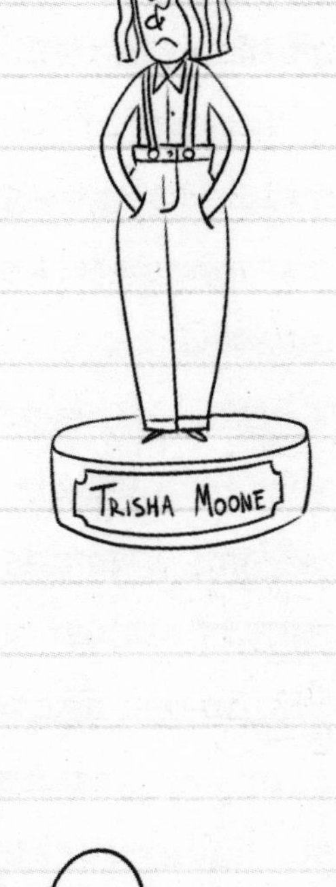

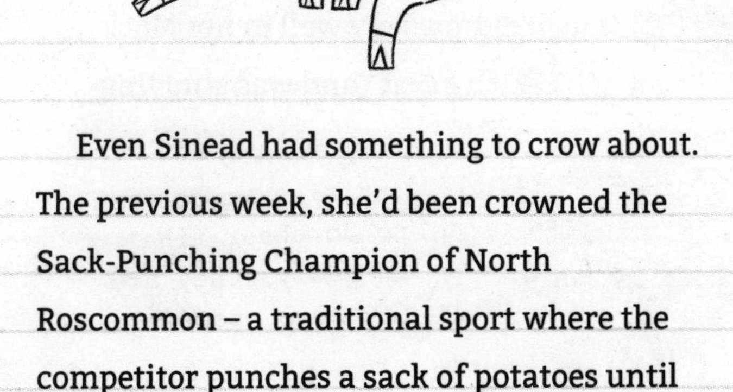

Even Sinead had something to crow about. The previous week, she'd been crowned the Sack-Punching Champion of North Roscommon – a traditional sport where the competitor punches a sack of potatoes until every spud has been mashed. The winner gets a sack of mashed potatoes. The loser gets *two* sacks of mashed potatoes.

Though they tried not to pick favourites, the Moone parents were clearly as proud as punch* of their triumphant trio. This had left Martin feeling a bit left out lately. Debra and Liam, his mam and dad, didn't often mention his failings, but the boy felt the sting of mediocrity around his sisters. He'd also felt the sting of Sinead's punches, which she insisted were an important part of her 'training'.

'Well, I think it's great that you're making a list, Martin,' Debra reassured him. 'You've always been a great man for writing down

*__PROUD AS PUNCH__ - punch is a fruit-based drink which is full of fruit. So it is, in fact, full of itself.

things you mean to get or do.'

'He has indeed!' agreed Liam. 'And who cares if they get done or get got? The most important thing is . . .' Liam's eyes narrowed as he looked more closely at his son's checklist. 'Martin, did you write that list of nonsense on the back of my chequebook?'

His sisters erupted in laughter.

'What a loser,' Sinead snorted.

'Hey!' Martin snapped, over the merry mayhem. 'OK, maybe I'm not a *winner* winner. Maybe I don't have any medals, or trophies, or certificates, or those lovely ribbons that they put on horses. Maybe I don't run fast enough or jump high enough or dance prettily enough. Maybe I'm no maths genius. Or geography genius. Or PE genius. Maybe sometimes I get to school and realize that I've forgotten to wear any underwear. And maybe I'm OK with that. Maybe I'm more comfortable knickerless.'

I felt Martin's speech was maybe going

off-piste*, so I whispered in his ear. 'Where are you going with this, buddy? You just seem to be making a list of all your failures. Maybe throw in some of your successes?'

He thought about this for a few long moments before saying, 'So in conclusion, I may not be a winner, but there's one thing I've always been, and that's—'

'A spanner?' suggested Sinead.

'A doer!' retorted Martin.

'Don't you mean a don'ter?' asked Trisha.

'Or a do-badly-er?' suggested Fidelma.

'I'm a doer! I'm a get-stuff-doner. I'm a *finisher*!' he declared, then stood up and waltzed off, leaving his breakfast unfinished.

***OFF-PISTE** – a skiing term, referring to a skier leaving the normal route of the slope. This often results in a collision, leaving the person in question piste-off.

CHAPTER TWO

WILBERT

Now hatted, coated and schoolbagged, Martin made his way towards school with his trusty wingman at his wing: me! Who wasn't coated or schoolbagged, but was identically hatted. Martin had given me my red, woolly hat when I first became his IF – his one and only prezzie to me. So far, at least . . .

And although he clearly wasn't the most *imaginative* gift-giver, I still hadn't given up hope. After all, this was only my first birthday in the imaginary employment of Martin Moone, so there was still time for him to surprise me with something special. And what I wanted more than anything was a pet.

So many of my friends had pets these days, and I was beyond jealous. Crunchie Haystacks had an adorable Grumbot, Loopy Lou had a fearsome Finkle, and even Bruce the Spruce had a fluffy Thudbottom, which slept in his branches all day and snarled at the stars all night. I didn't even mind what sort of pet I had – I just wanted a little companion to nuzzle me and bound around me, lick my face and nibble my toes after a hard day of IFing.

I'd dropped plenty of hints. I'd even cut out pictures from the pet section of *WHIF Magazine* and scattered them around – snaps of Bungletots, Whumps and a cute Skunkosaurus. But if Martin had seen them, he'd never mentioned it. And as we trudged down the narrow, winding road towards his school, he still seemed completely unaware that it was my birthday, having another morning moan about his sisters.

'How did I end up in a family of winners?' he

lamented. 'If anyone's a winner in our house, it should be me! I mean, look at me – I've got "winner" written all over me!'

I glanced at him, but the only thing written on him was the word 'plonker', which Sinead had scrawled on the back of his neck a couple of nights before, while Martin was sleeping. He'd tried to wash it off, but had only managed to smudge it, so it now looked more like 'plops'. But I decided not to remind Martin of his neck graffiti, keen to steer the conversation towards more important matters.

'Ahhhhh, I love this time of year!' I sighed happily. 'Spring is springing, hatchlings are hatching, chicks are . . . chicking – it's such a *birthy* time, isn't it? Spring days are the *birthiest days*!'

'It's so unfair!' Martin went on, completely missing my hint. 'I mean, what are they so good at? Cleverness? Artiness? Punchiness? That stuff is easy. What about the stuff *I'm* good at? Chattiness? Walkiness? Hattiness?' he said, patting his woolly hat. 'Where are my medals for those?'

I tried to jog his memory again. 'Look at that squirrel, Martin!' I cried, pointing at a tree. 'He's a jolly good fellow, isn't he?'

Martin frowned. 'Huh?'

'Yes, he's a jolly good fellow. *For he's a jolly good fellow! And so say all of us!*'

'It's just a squirrel, Sean.'

I watched it scamper away. 'There goes the happy guy!' I cried. 'But maybe he'll return to us some day. Many happy returns, squirrel! *Many. Happy. Returns!*'

'Since when do you like squirrels so much?' he asked. 'You usually call them "tree rats".'

'Do I? Well, I guess I'm feeling pretty squirrel-friendly right now because today's a special day.'

'Oh yeah? And why is it a—'

Suddenly Martin came to a halt, and looked at me in surprise.

'Holy moly!' he exclaimed. 'You're right,

Sean! How could I have forgotten?'

'How indeed!' I chuckled, relieved that the penny had finally dropped*.

'EOPS!' cried Martin.

'Sorry . . . ?'

'EOPS!' he repeated, sounding like a barking seal. 'EOPS, Sean! EOPS!'

'Are you having some kind of fit, Martin?'

'E-O-P-S! End-Of-Primary-School**!' he explained. 'It's exactly two months away!'

I rolled my eyes in despair. 'That's what you forgot?'

'You were right, Sean!' he continued excitedly. 'It's a special day all right. The end of an era! Another momentous milestone in the Martin Moone story. It's all change. We need to

***THE PENNY DROPPED** – when someone finally understands something. The phrase dates back to the time when our brains were coin-operated. To understand something, you'd drop a penny into your ear. Or if you were in maths class, you'd simply wedge your wallet up your nose.

****PRIMARY SCHOOL** – school from Junior-Trouser-Wetting to Can-Almost-Grow-A-Tache.

cherish these last walks, Sean – before SOSS.'

'Start-Of-Secondary-School*?' I guessed, with a sigh.

'Correcto, Beardo! After the summer, we'll be doing a *very slightly different* walk in the mornings. How nuts is that?'

I gave an unenthusiastic grunt.

'Aw, Sean, don't be sad about EOPS,' he said. 'Primary school is the past! We've gotta be like sharks – always swimming forward! Hunting the blood of New Experiences! Devouring the guts of Change For The Better!'

Suddenly he paused, staring into the bushes.

'Hey, what's that?'

'What's what?' I asked.

But he was already picking his way through the weeds, venturing off the road.

'Where are you going?' I asked, annoyed, as I followed after him.

***SECONDARY SCHOOL** – school from First Zits to First Ear Hair.

We made our way behind a leafy shrub, and there in the long grass we found a large wooden box! It was almost as tall as Martin, and we gazed at it in amazement.

'Wow!' he exclaimed. 'What's this?'

I frowned, peering at it. It was quite the mystery all right. 'Do you think it fell off a truck or something?' I wondered.

There was a strange smell coming from the box, and I began to walk around it curiously. Then I noticed something dangling from the lid.

'Wait – look. There's some kind of . . . tag!'

I gasped with shock. 'It's for me . . . ?!'

To Sean!
Happy Birthday to my BIF (Best Imaginary Friend)!
From your trusty Realsie,
Martin.
P.S. You can't return it because it has already soiled itself. Many times.

Martin was grinning from ear to ear. 'Well, you didn't think I forgot, did ya?'

I laughed. He'd got me all right, and I was impressed – it's not easy to fool someone who lives inside your head!

'Well, what are ya waiting for?' he cried. 'Open it up!'

I set upon the box excitedly and tried to lift up the heavy lid. I could hear loud snorting and snuffling coming from inside it, like a bull about to make his entrance at a rodeo. This was no hat. Something was alive in there! I lifted up the lid another inch and then – *SMASH!* – a wild-looking beast exploded out of it, leaping into the air and almost landing on top of us!

It was a shaggy-haired creature that was half werewolf and half donkey. It had a long donkey's face, but doggy ears and a couple of fangs for teeth. Its front legs had hoofs, but its back legs had paws, and on its belly was a patch of white fur with four tiny udders – which was odd since neither donkeys nor werewolves have udders. Or if they do, no one's ever dared to milk them. Its face had a slightly confused expression, as if it wasn't really sure which animal it was supposed to be – and as if to express this, it reared up on its hind paws and gave a deafening 'HEEE-HOOWWWWWLLLLL!'

'It's a Wonkey!' I cried with joy. 'My very own Wonkey!'

'His name is Wilbert,' announced Martin.

'I bought him on your day off, from some imaginary gypsies in a car park. They told me that "Wonkeys are an IF's Best Friend". Do you like him?'

'Like him? *I love him!*' I gushed, gazing into his big goofy eyes. 'Hello, Wilbert!'

The Wonkey grinned, and gave a belch. He bounded back to the box and plucked out a leash with his long mouth.

'Looks like he wants some exercise!' chuckled Martin.

Wilbert dropped the leash into my hand, along with a little handbook called *How to Care for Your Wonkey*.

'Good boy, Wilbert!' praised Martin. 'That's his manual, Sean. I think you're supposed to milk him at some point, but it explains it all in there.'

'Perfecto!' I cried, as I pocketed the book and strapped the leash to the collar of my furry new friend. 'I'm gonna take such good care of you, Wilbert! I'll walk you every day and snuggle you every night!'

I looked over at Martin, still hardly able to believe it. He'd really pulled this one out of the bag – or the box, as it were.

'Oh, Martin, I take it back, I take it *all* back! You're the best Realsie ever!' I proclaimed, and gave him a bear hug.

But a moment later, I was yanked out of his grip as the Wonkey tore off in a flash, dragging me along behind it, galloping away with another 'HEEE-HOOWWWWWWWLLLLLL!'

Martin watched us go, confused. 'Take *what* back?' he called after me, as I bounced along the road behind Wilbert.

CHAPTER THREE
THE WINNERS WALL

There's an old saying in the imaginary world that I once read on a tea towel in my granny's house:

I was pondering this mysterious nugget of wisdom as I tumbled and bumped my way down the Boyle Road after Wilbert.

Was I not showing him enough affection? I wondered. Was that why he was giving me this rough ride? I didn't want our friendship to start off on the wrong foot – or hoof, for that matter – so I tried yelling compliments at him in between my shrieks of pain.

'YOW! OOF! GOOD BOY! OUCH! ARRGH! WHO'S A HANDSOME WONKEY? OW! THAT WAS PRICKLY! WELL DONE!'

But no matter how much praise I hollered at him, I continued to bang, batter and bounce my way through the countryside like I was trapped inside a pinball machine made of roads. One mile and eighty-seven bruises later, Wilbert came to a sudden halt, panting happily. I smacked into his bum and he farted in my face – a fitting end to the worst journey of my life.

In a wobbly, stinky daze, I staggered to my feet, and saw that we'd reached the big yard outside Martin's school where crowds of kids were arriving, hurrying to get to class before the bell rang.

Every inch of my body was as sore as a savagely stubbed toe, but when Wilbert smiled up at me with his big toothy grin, my aches and pains melted away. How could I blame that big lovable dope? It wasn't *his* fault: Wonkeys weren't known for obedience. Or intelligence. Or pleasant body odour. They were known for being loyal and loving pets – 'An IF's Best Friend,' as Martin had said. Others called them 'Un-Toilet-Trainable Terrors' or 'Slobbery Snot Factories'. But not me, because I was a Wonkey-owner now, and I understood these noble creatures, I thought to myself, as I watched Wilbert run around in a circle, trying to bite his own buttocks.

'Ah, there ya are, Sean!' called Martin as he arrived at last. 'Still alive then?'

'Ah yes, just bonding with Wilbert here,' I chuckled, patting him on the nose. He didn't like that and gave a snarl, so I whipped my hand back, as casually as I could.

'Maybe I should've got you a *smaller* pet,' teased Martin. 'You sure you can handle him?'

I laughed. Martin clearly didn't know much about Wonkey-care – whereas I had been a Wonkey-owner for a solid seventeen minutes now and was pretty sure I knew what I was doing. 'It's not about *handling* him, Martin. It's about *understanding* him. *Trusting* him. *Connecting* with him.'

Martin nodded. 'You've got a pine cone in your hair.'

'Yep, I know.'

Just then we heard a voice hollering at us from across the yard. 'Hey, Martin!'

It was Padraic – Martin's round-faced, happy-headed best friend. He was waving excitedly out the window of a rusted bus that was parked beside the school. 'Hurry up! I got us some top-notch seats here! Only three chewing gums stuck to them! And loads of graffiti to read on the road!'

'Be right there, P!' Martin called, then turned back to us. 'Well, gang – are ya right?*'

***ARE YA RIGHT?** – Irish slang for 'Are you ready?' If you're not ready, then you might get left behind – so if you don't want to be left, then always be right.

But the Wonkey didn't seem right at all. He was smelling the air furiously like he'd caught some kind of delicious scent, and before I could leap on his leash, he galloped away like a shot.

'Wilbert!!' I wailed, watching him tear into school as the morning bell rang out.

A loud 'HEEE-HOOWWWWWWLLLLLL!' echoed through the corridor as we raced after the Wonkey, passing kids hurrying into their classrooms. Wilbert's howls were so loud that we thought for sure they must be able to hear him, but no one batted an eyelid as he bounded right past them.

Ahead of us, our old clown pal, Loopy Lou, came strolling out of Martin's classroom, on his way to join his Realsie Trevor on the bus. Wilbert skidded to a stop, and I crashed into his stinky rear end for the second time in five minutes as Martin tumbled over us both.

'Hey, guys! Almost forgot my snacky-snacks for the triperoo!' chirped Lou, as he munched on a bag of monkey nuts. 'Oooooh, a Wonkey!' he marvelled.

'He's mine! Isn't he adorable?' I gasped proudly, in a daze.

'He's a cutie-pie! Want a monkey nut, Wonkey-Donkey?'

Wilbert leaped hungrily at the bag, diving towards Lou with his sharp teeth bared.

'Argghhh!' yelped Lou, as he dropped his nuts, and fled as fast as he could, bumbling away in his over-sized clown shoes.

Wilbert pounced on the bag, and I pounced on his leash.

'Got him! Now let's get to that bus before

they leave without us!'

But Martin stayed put. He was still lying on the floor and was staring up at the wall beside us, with a wistful look. 'Ya know, Sean,' he said, a little sadly, 'I've passed this wall a million times, but I don't think I've ever really looked at it before.'

He got to his feet, gazing at the old trophies that were displayed there. Framed photographs showed students clutching silver cups and shiny medals, all celebrating various triumphs – sporting skill, academic accomplishments, musical magnificence, art artistry, maths mastery, chess championery and even bingo brilliance. They were all up there – the school's high-achievers, past and present, immortalized forever on The Winners Wall. But the face of Martin Moone was nowhere to be seen. Except on his own head, of course. Which was filled with disappointment now.

'I always thought I'd be up there some day, Sean. I've given this school so many years of my young life, and what do I have to show for it? Where is my face on that wall?!' he lamented.

Trying to perk him up, I pointed to a corner. 'There's a patch of mould there that kinda looks like you,' I offered helpfully. But Martin just sagged glumly.

'There's only two months left before EOPS. So I suppose I'll never be up there now,' murmured Martin. 'I'm in a house full of winners and a school full of winners. Where are all the losers?'

As if on cue, a sweaty-faced Padraic came charging down the corridor, with his imaginary friend, Crunchie 'Danger' Haystacks.

'Martin!' he blurted, out of breath. 'The bus – (*heave!*) – is about to – (*gasp!*) – go without ya!'

'Whoa! A Wonkey! What a beauty!' Crunchie said with admiration.

'He's mine, but if you share your bus-grub, I might let you pet him later,' I offered.

'Done!'

Martin snapped out of his sadness and hopped to his feet. 'Do we still have our primo seats?' he asked Padraic.

'Declan Mannion said he'd – (*wheeze!*) – mind them, so long as he could – (*pant!*) – write on them: "Reserved for two big arses". It seemed like a fair trade.'

'Nice work, P-Bomb. To the bus!'

I tugged on Wilbert's leash, and we all hightailed it back outside to the old, crockety coach.

'You're late, Moone!' snapped Martin's teacher, Mr Jackson, as we boarded the ancient rust-mobile. 'We've got a date with Science and she doesn't like to be kept waiting! So sit down, the pair of you! *Brostaígí, brostaígí!**'

TRANSLATION

'Chop-chop!'

I hoisted Wilbert into the luggage rack, wedging him in tightly. He gave a confused yowl as the boys scrambled into their freshly graffitied seats.

'Let's roll, Pat!' shouted Mr Jackson to the driver. 'The sooner we leave, the sooner we'll be back, and I'll be damned if I miss my step-aerobics class because of this lot!'

The bus roared into life as Pat the Driver steered us out of the school gates, and the whole class gave a cheer as we took to the open road, belching thick clouds of black smoke behind us.

CHAPTER FOUR
THE ROAD TO NOWHERE (BUT NEAR ROOSKY)

There's nothing I love more than driving through the beautiful lands of Roscommon. Watching the low sun sparkle off the surfaces of Lough Gara and Arrow. The rugged, rocky walls, as short and strong as the men who laid them. The lush, rolling hills that seem to gently caress the sky. Of course, I couldn't see any of that stuff, because I was crammed into an overhead luggage rack with two bonkers IFs and a farty Wonkey. The racks were so small, shy goldfish would have felt claustrophobic* in them.

***CLAUSTROPHOBIC** – a fear of confined spaces. The word 'phobia' comes from the Greek word for 'fear'. 'Claus', of course, refers to Santa. The term 'claustrophobia' was first coined when an elf named Agamemnon found himself trapped inside Santa's sack the day after Christmas. It was a long year for the poor fella.

We were on the road to the mysterious science place. Below us, the chaotic bus was a tangle of limbs and songs and calls and falls.

Crunchie had decided that it was a good time to count his body freckles; Loopy Lou was whistling a song backwards, believing it would help his motion sickness. Wilbert was squeezed so tightly into the rack that his 'Heeee-Hooowwwwls' had become quite high pitched. This made him sound like a helium-hungry hen. But at least he couldn't escape, and as we drove up and down the rocky country roads, I fed him more monkey nuts while reading my Wonkey handbook.

'Those are *my* nuts!' complained Lou.

'Well, he's grateful that you dropped them, Lou. Aren't ya, Willy?' I asked, tossing him another one.

He gobbled it up, and Lou shook his head with annoyance before going back to his reverse-whistle.

'Oooh, this is interesting,' I said, as I read

aloud: *'Although they adore monkey nuts, most Wonkeys are violently allergic to them.* That's odd, isn't it? I wonder why they . . .'

I could feel Lou staring at me as I fed Wilbert another fistful of nuts.

'Oh,' I said, realizing my mistake. 'You think I should probably stop fee—'

'Aaaaatttcceeewwwhhhooowwwwl' Wilbert

blurted, as he sneezed all over Loopy Lou. Actually, it's not right to call it a sneeze. It was more like a giant nose spit. Either way, Lou wasn't delighted about it. Wilbert's stomach gave an unhappy gurgle, and I decided to tuck the monkey nuts out of sight for the rest of the journey.

Below us, the bus was in chaos. The song 'N17' by The Saw Doctors was being hollered by the group with the pride of the national anthem. It was a song about a road – the actual road we were on. The Bonner brothers were stamping their feet in time, either performing the drum section or trying to smash a hole in the floor of the bus. It was really hard to tell.

Trevor, sitting alone in the seat in front of them, seemed to find the stomping unpleasant. Like Lou, Trevor was prone to motion sickness. His face had taken on the colour of the green countryside we were meandering through. He clutched his schoolbag close to his chest, ready in case his nausea got physical. Down at the back, Declan Mannion was having a glorious time. He was looking out the window, making rude hand gestures at drivers who honked back angrily, which seemed to please Declan no end.

'Ha! Stupid cars!' He laughed, as though it was them and not the drivers he'd been offending all along.

Martin and Padraic were sitting happily together playing mind-agility games. They were on their fifth round of How Many Fingers Am I Holding Up Behind My Back? The score was delicately poised at 2–2. But I think we all know that game has no real winner. The deciding round was interrupted by Mr Jackson.

'Would you stop that carry-on, Mannion!'

A small car containing a trio of young nuns in tears passed by the bus. They were gesturing towards Declan, who'd clearly just offended them.

'Declan, this is your umpteenth* class trip – don't you know better than that by now?!' yelled the irate teacher.

'How many years d'ya think Declan has been in school?' Martin asked Padraic.

His buddy shrugged. 'I heard Declan was the one who actually *built* our school.'

'Some say that he's the ghost of a former janitor,' Martin whispered.

'I heard Declan is so old that on his first class trip, they travelled on horseback,' interjected Trevor from the seat behind.

'My dad says Declan looks like his old PE teacher,' added Padraic.

'They'll never let him go to secondary school if he keeps failing everything. I bet he'll spend his whole life stuck in sixth class, the big eejit!' giggled Trevor.

***UMPTEENTH** – a number without a number. Its actual value is a mystery. Although it's probably high. Or low.

'Would that be so bad?' Martin asked, defending him. 'At least he'll be remembered.'

The boys looked to Martin for explanation.

'Declan was the first person to graffiti the *inside* of a teacher's hat. The first person to steal every spoon from the canteen. The first person to set up a union of primary school kids, then make them strike for a month for free custard,' Martin said respectfully. 'But what will *I* be remembered for?'

As Padraic and Trevor sat silently thinking for an uncomfortably long time, a strange sound came from the front of the battered old bus.

'Ah brr***uughh**itwe!' yelled Pat the Driver.

'Watch your language in front of the students, Pat,' Mr Jackson warned.

Pat the Driver hastily pulled the bus over to the side of the road, and it sputtered to a stop.

'Not cursing, Mr J – just sayin' we're gonna be stuck here. The thing's busted.'

'What thing?'

'The flippin' brr***uughh**itwe!'

Already feeling like his life was going nowhere, Martin slowly disembarked by a ditch in the middle of nowhere.

CHAPTER FIVE
THE BUSTED BUS

Martin's class had de-bussed from the busted bus and were waiting in the middle of the quiet road while Mr Jackson gave out to* Pat the Driver, who was examining the exhausted engine.

I'd decided to let Wilbert stretch his legs and was watching him bound around the fields like an overexcited, massively misshapen puppy. Crunchie Haystacks was trying to teach him to play 'fetch' with a stick, but the Wonkey ignored the stick and kept fetching Loopy Lou instead.

***GAVE OUT TO** – this might sound generous, but it just means 'yelled at'. The Irish are a very charitable people, so even when they shout at someone, it's described like it's a gift.

Beside the bus, Lou's Realsie, Trevor, wasn't feeling too happy either. 'I wonder how long we'll be stranded like this,' he grumbled to Martin and Padraic. 'It's getting chilly.'

'Well, it's only going to get chillier, Trev,' warned Padraic as he squinted up at the sky. 'By my calculations, we've got about twelve minutes until sundown.'

Martin glanced at his watch. 'It's only ten in the morning, Padraic.'

'OK, then we've got loads of time. Good stuff!'

'Everyone stay calm!' shouted Mr Jackson, marching over to the boys. 'We're all going to be fine, so no one needs to flip out!'

The boys all looked at him blankly. 'We're not flipping out, sir,' said Martin.

'I said calm down, Moone!' shouted his red-faced teacher. 'Everyone just take a deep breath, OK? No one's going to miss the science trip! And no one's going to miss their step-aerobics class!'

'What's the plan, Jermaine?' asked Declan Mannion. 'Want me to rob a tractor?'

'Don't call me by my first name!' snapped Mr Jackson. 'And there'll be no robbing of tractors. Not yet anyway. We simply need to hitch a lift.' He counted the heads around him. 'In about nine cars.'

'But what if nine cars don't stop for us?' asked Jonner Bonner.

'Well, then we might need to hunker down

for a bit,' admitted their teacher. 'If it starts raining, we'll need to find some kind of shelter,' he said, scanning their surroundings for a barn or a tree or a big cave.

'We could just get back in the bus,' suggested Martin.

'Perfect!' exclaimed Mr Jackson. 'That's shelter sorted. So all we'll need is food.'

'There's some berries over here!' called Conor Bonner, who was standing beside a bush.

'Right, everyone eat some of those berries!' ordered their teacher.

The class looked a bit hesitant, wondering if the berries might be poisonous, but the Bonners were already stuffing their mouths.

'Can we just eat our packed lunches instead?' asked Trevor. 'My mum made me some lovely crêpes*.'

***CRÊPES** – pancakes. There's a little hat on the 'E' because it's a French word, and most French words like to wear stylish hats – unlike Swedish words who prefer to balance apples on their heads – Ö.

Mr Jackson was just about to yell at him when Pat the Driver called, 'Eh, Mr J? That science place is just over there!'

He was pointing towards a large building behind a tree, and Mr Jackson brightened.

'Good news! It seems that Pat the Driver hasn't *completely* ruined our science trip! We shall finish our journey on foot!' he declared, and marched off down the road towards the building. 'Keep up now! Brostaígí, brostaígí!'

The Bonner brothers spat out their mouthfuls of possibly poisonous berries, and hurried after the others. I gave a shrill whistle to the Wonkey, which he completely ignored. But once Lou started running my way, Wilbert followed, and we left the stranded bus behind with Pat the Driver, who looked very relieved to be abandoned by everyone and was now unwrapping a much-needed Bounty bar*.

***BOUNTY BAR** – also known as 'the taste of paradise'. Unless you're allergic to coconuts or chocolate, in which case it's the taste of dangerous swelling, cold sweats and a short stay in hospital.

Mr Jackson had kept their destination a secret, so as the class approached, their excitement was building.

'I've never been on a science trip before,' said Padraic feverishly. 'I wonder what wonders we're about to see!'

'Rocket boots?' suggested Martin, eagerly. 'Robot ninjas? Time-travelling trampolines?'

'Space chocolate? Alien toffee? Computer sandwiches?' squealed Padraic, who was clearly getting hungry.

But before they could wonder some more, Mr Jackson came to a halt outside the main gates. 'Behold!' he shouted, gesturing at a large sign in front of them. 'We are here at last!'

Martin read the sign with confusion. 'The Roscommon Museum . . . of *Tractors?*'

'Is it *behind* this place?' asked Padraic hopefully.

'It *is* this place, Padraic. We have reached our destination!' proclaimed their teacher proudly.

The entire class sagged with disappointment,

and there were grumbles of 'I should've flippin' well known', 'I can see stupid tractors at home' and 'I wish we'd swallowed those poisonous berries'.

Mr Jackson pretended not to hear their moans. 'That's right, gang! The one and only Roscommon Museum of—'

HONNNNNNNNKKKKK!

His voice was drowned out by the arrival of a huge bus, and Mr Jackson leaped back into a muddy puddle to get out of its way. Several gasps were heard, as this bus was like none we'd ever seen before. Brand new, ultra-modern, and completely dirtless, it was the colour of money – a sleek, shiny silver – and it glittered like one of the trophies on the Winners Wall. Through its windows we could see well-groomed students with blow-dried hair and soft, make-upped faces. They peered down with mild amusement at Martin and his dishevelled friends who gawked up at them from the mud below. As the bus crept past, it belched fumes in our faces that smelt like warm caramel.

'Now *that's* a bus,' I sighed.

'Flippin' posh school!' griped Mr Jackson, as he splashed out of the puddle. Then he spotted a sign for the toilets. 'Right, gang, who needs the loo?'

Almost every hand went up.

'OK, let's get in there quick before that other bus parks. Go, go, go!'

Everyone charged off, and I turned to Martin who was left standing there, alone.

'You don't need to pee, buddy?' I asked, in disbelief. 'You *always* need to pee.'

'Believe me, I'm as surprised as you are, Sean. Must be because of all that sherbet I ate on the bus. It tends to absorb every drop of liquid in my body.'

'Maybe we should've given Wilbert some sherbet too,' I muttered, as we watched him generously marking his territory around the museum.

I should say that calling this place a 'museum' was a bit of a stretch. It was little more than a big shed, or a barn. In fact, I think it actually *was* a barn, as we noticed a few hens fluttering out the back door. But the words 'MUSEUM – *not* a barn' were painted on its side to avoid any confusion, and there were some flowers planted around it, which Wilbert was busy watering. He dashed out of sight, and then we heard a whimper, followed by a booming voice:

'Whose Wonkey is this? Whose Wonkey just peed on the pansies?!'

We hurried over to find a large-bellied, bushy-bearded man holding Wilbert by his ears. He was imaginary, but not an IF like myself, as he seemed to be employed by the museum instead of by a Realsie, judging by his friendly name tag and unfriendly expression.

'Eh, he's mine,' I confessed.

'Curb your Wonkey, sir!' he boomed at me.

I nodded, unsure what he meant, and took hold of Wilbert, who looked petrified.

'Are you here for the tour?' he asked me.

Martin and I shared a confused look. 'I'm here for *his* tour,' I explained. 'About . . . tractors?'

'What about the imaginary tour?' demanded the man.

'There's an imaginary tour?' asked Martin, curious.

'Of course there's an imaginary tour! Every museum in the world has an imaginary tour! You think Realsies got anything done without their imaginary friends? The Realsie tour is about great Realsies; the imaginary tour is about great IFs. Ready to start?'

'Ehhh . . .'

'Magnificent! I shall be your guide. The name is Brendan. Brendan McSnozz!' He then noticed Crunchie wandering around behind us. 'You're coming too, are you, my wrestler friend?'

'Who – me?' asked Crunchie.

'Excellent. And you can mind the Wonkey, Clown Man.'

'Do what?' asked a bewildered Lou.

'This way, this way,' cried Brendan, ushering Crunchie and me into the tractor museum.

Martin went to follow us, but Brendan stopped him. 'Sorry, my boy. Realsies go on the Realsie tour.'

'Oh.'

And with that, he whisked us inside and slammed the door shut with a loud *boom!*

CHAPTER SIX
ST WHIMMION'S AND THE MAD MECHANIC

As Crunchie and I followed Brendan McSnozz through the exhibits, another tour guide – a real one – was outside greeting the new arrivals. Martin's class were still on their toilet trip, but the posh kids were disembarking from the silver bus, wearing snazzy blazers that bore the crest of their private school.

'Welcome, St Whimmion's!' said the plump, smiling tour guide. 'My name is Moira. Are we ready to venture into the wonderful world of tractors?'

She paused for a cheer, but the grumpy group took one glance at the museum and looked immediately bored. There were mutters of 'When are we going back to Dublin?', 'There'd better be video games in there', and

'I need another cappuccino'.

'Yes we are, Moira!' Moira replied to herself with a chuckle. 'Now let's get a headcount!'

She proceeded to count their soft, perfumed heads as one of them, a sharp-nosed girl named Veronica, put on a pair of stylish sunglasses – even though the sun wasn't shining and had not actually shone for two months and six days.

She noticed Martin smelling the bus nearby, savouring the whiff of caramel.

'Are you the tea boy?' she asked.

Martin looked startled. 'What? Eh. No, I'm the . . . Moone boy.'

She pointed at him. 'Hey, look everyone – it's one of the locals! Are you from the Country?'

'The country?'

'The Country!'

'*This* country?' asked a confused Martin. 'Don't let my tanned complexion fool ya!' he chuckled, pointing at his face, which was about as tanned as a jar of mayonnaise. 'I am indeed from Ireland.'

'Not the country. *The Country.*'

Martin looked flummoxed. 'Oh, you mean the . . . *countryside*? No, I'm from a town. Called Boyle. The greatest town in Ireland!'

'Is it in Dublin?'

'No.'

'Then you're from the Country.'

'Oh,' said Martin, even more befuddled. It seemed that a Dubliner's map of Ireland was a lot emptier than regular maps.

'Anyhoo . . . Welcome to *Outside Dublin*. Martin Moone's the name.'

'I'm Vronny,' she replied, 'and this is my boyfriend, Max.'

A handsome boy with spiky blond hair smirked at Martin. 'Hey, Marty – what's happenin'?'

Martin was unsure how to answer this. Wasn't it obvious what was happening? He was talking to Vronny. But then he thought, maybe Max was a bit simple. That might explain why his shirt collars were pointing straight up. Martin looked him over, but nothing else was backwards. Just upside-down collars. It reminded him of the time Padraic's dog came back from the vet wearing a large cone around his neck. Was this a similar safety measure? Surely Max wasn't in danger of licking stitches off his bum? But then again, Martin had never met people from Dublin before . . .

'You here for the tour?' asked Max through his pointy collars. 'Or do you live in that barn?'

Martin glanced at the museum behind them. 'Eh. No, I'm here for the tour. But my class are all in the loo. They wanted to beat you to it.'

'They needn't have bothered,' scoffed Vronny. 'We've got lots of loos on board.'

'And a bath,' added Max.

'A *bath*? On a *bus*?!' gasped Martin.

'And a pastry chef.'

Martin was flabbergasted. 'So . . . hang on. You're saying that you can *order a cake*. And eat it *in the bath*? *On the bus*?'

'Can't you do that on your bus?' asked Vronny.

Martin thought of the busted bus with its holes, graffiti and chewing-gummed seats. But then he remembered that there was a dip in the floor around the third row, where rainwater sometimes gathered, having leaked through the roof.

'Yeah, we've . . . *kinda* got a bath,' answered Martin vaguely. 'I suppose I could eat my sandwiches in it on the way home.'

Just then, a damp-haired teacher hopped off the silver bus, smelling like lavender and warm butter.

'Sorry, gang – didn't realize we'd arrived! I was just in the tub having a quick croissant*. Are we all set?'

Vronny turned to Martin. 'Want to join us on the tour? Or are you gonna wait for your toilet friends?'

***CROISSANT** - long ago, a boy annoyed his mum's sister, so she flung a piece of dough at him. It landed in the oven, got accidentally cooked, and turned into a delicious pastry - which the boy named after his 'cross aunt'. (He also invented a tart called a 'clumsy uncle', but it was less successful.)

'Eh . . .' murmured Martin, unsure.

'Hey, Hugh!' called Max.

Their teacher, who apparently didn't mind being called 'Hugh', strode over to Martin with a fascinated look, like Max had just discovered a strange local insect.

'What have you got there, Maxo?' he asked, peering at Martin.

'Mind if we let this mucker* join us on the tour, Hugh?' asked Vronny.

'I think you mean, can *we* join this mucker on *his* tour? This is bogland, Vronzer. We're in *his* neck of the woods.'

Hugh beamed at Martin. 'What do you say? Can we join you?'

Martin was a bit baffled, but just shrugged. 'Can I have an eclair afterwards? In the bus-bath?'

Hugh grinned. 'It's a deal, little man.'

And with that, Martin and the rich kids all

***MUCKER** - a city dweller's name for a rural person. A rural person's name for a city dweller is a 'Mr Clean Boots'.

followed Moira into the museum, passing the Wonkey, who was happily gnawing on a pair of clown shoes while a barefoot Loopy Lou tiptoed away, quietly abandoning the clueless creature.

The museum left a lot to be desired. There were a few photos on the wall and some old bits of farm machinery lying around, while the odd goat wandered between rooms. But Martin enjoyed Moira's tour. The highlight was an exhibit about an Irish inventor called Harry Ferguson. His nickname was 'The Mad Mechanic', and he led quite a life. He started out as a bicycle repairman, but loved to tinker with engines, and invented all sorts of contraptions. He built motorbikes, made the first ever four-wheel-drive Formula-One racing car, and he even invented his own aeroplane.

'Harry Ferguson wanted to be the first Irishman to fly,' Moira told them. 'He crashed his plane hundreds of times, but kept fixing it and trying again, determined to reach his dream before the end of the year 1909. But by late December, he still hadn't done it. The weather was brutal, and all seemed lost. But he decided to make one last attempt.'

'I've been on a plane!' yelled out Max. 'Flying is easy!'

There were murmurs of agreement from his classmates.

'Yeah, you just sit there.'

'I ate pretzels!'

Only Martin seemed captivated. 'So did he do it?' he asked Moira.

She winked at him and led him over to a display where there was a framed page from the *Belfast Telegraph*. She read out one of the paragraphs:

'The machine was set against the roaring wind, but the splendid pull of the new propeller swept the big aeroplane along as Mr Ferguson advanced the lever. The plane rose into the air at nine, and then twelve feet, amidst the hearty cheers of the onlookers. The poise of the machine

was perfect and, despite fierce gusts of wind, Mr Ferguson made a splendid flight of 130 yards!'

'Wow!' exclaimed Martin, mightily impressed as he gazed at the picture of Ferguson soaring through the sky.

'I thought this was a tractor museum! Why are we talking about planes?' griped Max.

'Yeah, good point, Maxo,' added his teacher.

'Because,' continued Moira, 'Harry Ferguson also invented tractors. He made the original Ferguson tractor in 1926 that is the same basic design for all tractors used today, and his name lives on in the Massey Ferguson company. He helped to transform farm machinery from horse-drawn contraptions into modern machines, like this one, my favourite of all his inventions: *The Black Tractor.*'

She gestured to a dark, sleek contraption that glistened in the shadows, and even the rich kids were impressed.

'Ooooooh.'

Martin had never heard of an Irish inventor before, but here was one who'd invented tractors, motorbikes, racing cars and aeroplanes! And he even had a cool nickname. There was a fella in Boyle called 'The Peculiar Plumber' who could fix a leaky toilet with just a rubber band and a wad of earwax – but 'The Mad Mechanic' was even more inspiring!

CHAPTER SEVEN
BARNEY BUNTON AND THE INVENTION CONVENTION

'Behind every great Realsie is a great IF!' boomed Brendan McSnozz at the end of the imaginary tour. 'And each of these incredible inventors had an imaginary friend looking over their shoulder. When they failed, their IFs bucked them up. When they were flummoxed, their IFs unflummoxed them. And when they succeeded, it was their IFs who cheered the loudest. Without them, would any inventor have made anything?!' he demanded, staring at us with great intensity.

Crunchie glanced at me. 'Is he asking *us* that?'

'Don't interrupt!' bellowed Brendan, and Crunchie jumped with fright.

'Now, where was I? Ah yes! Would the tractor

have become the greatest vehicle on Earth without the help of IFs? And what about other inventions? Popcorn pillows? Doggie coffee? Shoe umbrellas? And would Harry Ferguson have soared through the skies without Barney Bunton at his side? WHO KNOWS?!' he cried out, raising his arms dramatically.

He then gave a low, theatrical bow, and dropped a little smoke bomb on to the ground. A white cloud billowed up from it, and Brendan disappeared from view.

Crunchie burst into applause. 'Wow! What a finish!'

'Wait!' I called. But Brendan had completely vanished. 'I had a question!'

Brendan popped out of a little cupboard where he'd been hiding. 'Oh. What is it?'

'Who's Barney Bunton?'

Brendan's eyes twinkled. 'Ah! The great Barney Bunton.'

He grasped my shoulder firmly (a little *too* firmly) and led me to a display where there was a framed page from an old newspaper. 'Now *there* was a brilliant IF! Imaginary friend to the great inventor Harry Ferguson,' he said, gesturing at the photo.

It showed a man flying an aeroplane while a delighted-looking IF stood behind him, waving his cap with glee.

Belfast Telegraph

THE MAD MECHANIC TAKES TO THE AIR

'There was nothing that he and Harry couldn't solve; nothing they couldn't invent! They were quite the pair, Harry and Barney – inseparable right up until the end. But we've still got something to remember Barney by.'

He gestured behind him towards a silver hook on the wall.

'His trusty cap.'

'What cap?' I asked.

Brendan turned to the hook, which was empty.

'It's gone!' gasped Brendan. 'It's been stolen! Our most prized possession! The greatest— Oh wait – there it is,' he said, pointing to a different hook, which held an old cap. 'I forgot we moved it to that hook. Any other questions?'

Crunchie looked at him curiously. 'You seem to like IFs a lot. Don't you want to be one, instead of an imaginary tour guide?'

'Ha! And spend my days stuck with a snotty little Realsie?' chuckled Brendan. 'I don't know how you do it, gentlemen. I tip my hat to thee.'

He tipped his hat respectfully and then suddenly raised his arms again. 'And now our tour is CONCLUDED!'

He hurled another smoke bomb at the ground, but this one didn't go off, and just rolled under a tractor.

'Flippin' cheap smoke bombs,' he muttered.

Brendan squeezed back into the cupboard, opened his lunchbox, and quietly shut the door.

I turned back to the old newspaper where Barney stood on the plane waving his cap in the air.

When Martin had looked at the photo on his tour, he saw no sign of Barney Bunton – and the reason for this is very simple. Martin could see almost everything in the imaginary world – in the last year, he'd met talking trees, chocolate fish, a magnificent magpie and, most recently, our imaginary tour guide. But there was one thing he couldn't see: another Realsie's IF. Why was that? Because they didn't exist in Martin's head. Other IFs lived in the imaginations of other people. And since Barney was Harry's IF, Martin couldn't see him in the photo. Only IFs can see other IFs.

I was trying to decide if being able to see other IFs was a blessing or a curse as I watched Crunchie's hairy belly bound and jiggle towards me in his skimpy wrestling outfit.

'They've got an imaginary gift shop!' he exclaimed, and handed me a little brown bag. 'Happy birthday, Sean.'

'Aww, Crunchie.' I smiled, incredibly touched, while also thinking, *About flippin' time!*

I opened the bag and pulled out a little vehicle with two bright lights that turned on when you pressed a button.

'What's this?' I asked, turning on the light. 'Some kind of . . . tractor-shaped torch?'

Crunchie nodded, grinning. 'It's called a Tractor Beam!'

He giggled, but I just frowned. 'I don't get it.'

'A Tractor Beam! Like in *Star Wars* – when

they use a tractor beam to pull a spaceship towards them. But this is just a tractor. With a beam.'

I nodded slowly. And gradually I realized that this was in fact the funniest thing ever!

We laughed for a solid six minutes.

*

Later, Martin followed Moira back outside with the kids from St Whimmion's. He glanced around for his classmates, but there was still no sign of them.

'So that concludes our tour,' Moira told them, with slightly less fanfare than Brendan McSnozz. 'But if any of you are feeling inspired and would like to make an invention of your own, there's a big competition coming up soon. It's a lot of fun, and there's medals and trophies for the winners.'

Martin's ears pricked up. *Medals? Trophies?* That was exactly the kind of thing he needed to get a place on the Winners Wall! And she said 'soon' – how soon? Was it something he could actually win before . . .

'EOPS?!' he blurted out in a panic.

Everyone looked at him.

'Sorry?' asked Moira.

'Oh. Eh. I meant . . . *Tell me more.*'

'Well, it's called the Invention Convention,'

she explained, 'and it's for young scientists like yourselves. Would anyone like an application—'

'Max and I have already entered!' interrupted Vronny. 'And we're totally going to win.'

'We sure are!' chuckled her teacher. 'I mean – *they* are. Because teachers aren't allowed to help. Which is why I'm not. Helping. Or hiring professional scientists to do the work. Because that's also banned. Which is why I'm not doing that either.'

Hugh stopped talking. He was sweating slightly, and he glanced around uneasily.

'I'll take an application!' piped up Martin.

Moira handed him a form as Max and Vronny scoffed.

'Do you even *have* science in the Country?' sneered Max.

'More like Sty-ence!' chimed in Vronny.

Martin looked at her blankly.

'Cos it smells like a pigsty,' she explained.

Max laughed, but Martin scowled. He'd had

just about enough of all their countryside-bashing.

'You know, just because you live in the city doesn't mean you're better than us,' he snapped.

'You sure about that?' asked Max doubtfully.

'I'm . . . mostly sure, yes! We might not have a bus that's filled with profiteroles*, but we're just as clever as you lot, and we'll easily beat you in that Invention Convention!'

Max and Vronny burst out laughing.

'You're going to beat *us*?!' jeered Vronny. 'With your invention of what? Muck burgers? Potato hats? Pointy spears?'

'We're not a bunch of savages, you know!' retorted Martin.

Just then, Moira spotted an approaching

***PROFITEROLES** – cream-filled, chocolate-covered pastry puffs. If you feel that the one downside to an eclair is that you can't quite jam it all into your mouth in one go, then say hello to profiteroles!

group. 'Ah, the boys from Boyle – just in time for the next tour!'

Unfortunately for Martin, his teacher and classmates happened to look *exactly* like a bunch of savages at that moment. They were munching large turkey legs, with their faces covered in ketchup, and their clothes were ripped and dishevelled.

'Where were you, Martin?' called Padraic. 'We wanted a snack, and Declan found a place that sells turkey legs! But we had to climb through a thorny ditch to get there!' He held up a bone that he'd been gnawing. 'Want some?'

Vronny and the others sniggered at the sight of the Country cavemen. 'What was that about not being savages?' she jeered.

The rich kids sauntered back to their sweet-smelling bus and climbed aboard.

'You just wait!' shouted Martin, as the rest of the St Whimmion's crew hopped up the steps. 'I'll build the greatest invention ever! I'll wipe the floor with you lot!'

Hugh smirked at him. 'Sure ya will, Marty. Sure ya will.'

'Oh, you'd better believe it. And now, if you'll stand aside, I'd like to take my pastry bath.'

Hugh closed the door in his face, and the St Whimmion's bus drove off, leaving behind the scent of freshly baked flapjacks and the sound of 'Ghostbusters 2' playing on their in-bus entertainment system.

'Hey, buddy. What did I miss?'

Martin turned to see me standing beside him.

He opened his mouth to answer, but I stopped him. 'Ya know what? Tell me later. In great detail – so I can put it all in the book!'

'I said curb your Wonkey!' yelled a familiar voice.

We turned to see Brendan chasing Wilbert away from the pansies. It seemed that Loopy Lou had done a runner.

'Oh balls,' I muttered.

'Come here, you weak-bladdered beast!' ordered Brendan, but the Wonkey sprinted away and darted through the main doors of the museum with Brendan hot on his heels.

'Wilbert!' I shrieked, as Martin and I raced after them.

CHAPTER EIGHT

N.P.

A loud 'HEEE-HOOWWWWWWWLLLLLL!' reverberated through the museum-barn. We scrambled after the sound, following it to the main exhibit area, and when we got there we found Brendan wrestling the Wonkey on the floor.

'Get off, ya big . . . slobbering . . . jackanapes*!' he grunted, as the Wonkey licked his face and sucked on his beard.

'Just play dead! He'll lose interest eventually!' I called to Brendan, remembering a tip from my Wonkey handbook.

***JACKANAPES** – a cheeky monkey. You might think it should be 'jackanape', but it isn't. It's one jackanapes. Two jackanapeses. Three jackanupials. And that's it – there's never been more than three.

But they continued to wrestle.

'Give it back!' Brendan boomed. 'Give it back, I say!'

'Give what back?' I asked.

'The cap! Barney Bunton's cap! The silly beast just ate it!' wailed Brendan. 'I knew we should have left it on the old hook.'

'Who's Barney Bunton?' asked Martin blankly.

'*Who's Barney Bunton?!*' snapped an exasperated Brendan.

'Don't worry!' I called. 'Wilbert has a very delicate stomach. We'll have that cap back in a jiffy.'

I dug in my pockets, pulled out some monkey nuts, and offered them to Wilbert. He immediately sprang to his feet and gobbled them up. Then sure enough, just a moment later, his stomach started gurgling again.

Brendan was now free from the Wonkey, but his mood had not improved. 'That hat was priceless!' he fumed, 'It was our sole link to the great—'

'I'd stand back if I were you,' I suggested.

Brendan paused, and then retreated from the Wonkey.

'Aaaaatttcceeewwwhhhooowwwwl!' Wilbert sneezed, splattering a wet gob of mucus on the floor.

But he wasn't done yet. He'd eaten too many monkey nuts for that. More gurgles were emanating from his insides. He looked quite pale and was doing lots of little burps. Then he perked up and seemed much happier. Then he looked sleepy. Then he seemed confused. And then he barfed all over the room.

It was an *extraordinary* amount of puke. And floating in the middle of this steaming stew was Barney Bunton's cap.

'Good heavens,' murmured Brendan. 'I'll . . . get the mops.' He stumbled out of the room in a state of shock.

Wilbert gave a sigh of relief, much happier

now, and bounded away with a cheeky wink, leaving a trail of wet puke-steps behind him.

I picked up the famous cap, which was in quite a sorry state. I gave it a shake and tried to scoop out the goop from inside it – when I felt something and paused.

It was a lump. A lump inside the hat.

I ran my finger over it, curious, and saw that there was a hidden fold in the fabric, like a little pocket. A secret pocket.

Why would Barney Bunton have a secret pocket in his cap?

I reached inside and pulled out a small, green glass bottle. It was like a medicine bottle with an old faded label stuck to the glass.

'What is it?' asked Martin, peering over my shoulder.

'N.P.' I murmured.

'N.P.?' he asked. 'What's N.P.?'

But that was all the label said. Just those two letters: N.P.

We were both wondering what this could possibly mean when Brendan clattered back with armfuls of mops and buckets. He looked over towards the cap in my hands, worried. 'Well?'

'Good as new!' I lied.

I tossed him the soggy hat, but decided not to mention our discovery, and quietly pocketed the glass bottle.

'You stole it?' whispered a shocked Martin when we were back outside.

'I just borrowed it,' I assured him. 'And besides – Brendan didn't even know he had it! You can't steal something from someone who doesn't know that the something you're stealing from them even exists!'

'Huh?'

'I'll return it later,' I promised. 'But not until we've solved its mystery.'

Martin gave a reluctant smile, and we strolled off to rejoin his classmates.

A few hours later, we were back home in Boyle. I'd filled Martin in about the imaginary tour, and after I'd walked Wilbert, fed him a dandelion cake, and sung him to sleep, we sat in Martin's bedroom, staring at the bottle again.

'N.P. . . .' I murmured, as we peered into the green glass.

'*Not Pizza?*' suggested Martin.

'Well, it's definitely not pizza.'

'*Nor Pandas?*'

'Nope, it's not pandas either.

'*Nothing Perhaps?*'

'It's definitely *something*, Martin.'

We hadn't been brave enough to open the bottle yet, but we could see something inside it.

'*Noodle Perfume?*' suggested Martin. '*Nut Pipe? News Paper?*'

'Martin, are you just saying any N.P. words that pop into your head?'

'Neck Pancakes?'

'I'm not sure this is *super* helpful, buddy.'

'Namby Pamby? Night Paint? Nail Polish?'

'OK, just stop! Actually . . . Nail polish – that comes in little bottles too. Maybe it *is* nail polish.'

'Only one way to find out, Sean.'

'What's that?'

'Time to paint our nails!'

I scratched my beard. 'Hmmm. That's probably not the *only* way to find out – but it's definitely the most fun! And these old mitts of mine could do with a dash of colour. Let's open it up!'

I pulled out the cork and peered inside. Whatever was in there, it wasn't a liquid. I tipped the bottle into my hand, and out fell several dried-up fragments, like ancient, shrivelled raisins.

'What are they?' wondered Martin.

I picked up a few and popped them into my mouth.

'Mmm. Crunchy,' I noted, munching on

them. But as they got wet, they became rather more slimy. I swallowed and was left with a revolting taste on my tongue.

We were still no closer to the truth.

Just then, Fidelma marched in with a stack of books.

'Out,' she ordered. 'I need this room to study.'

'But . . . this is my bedroom,' protested Martin, a bit taken aback.

'It's not your bedroom – it's Sinead's too,' pointed out Fidelma.

'Fine. It's *half* my bedroom. So get out of my half.'

'No can do. I'm sick of studying in my bedroom. So I'm studying here now,' she insisted, dropping her books on to Martin's bed.

'Ow!' he yelped, diving away from the book avalanche. 'Why can't you study in Sinead's half?'

'I prefer your half. There's fewer holes in the walls.'

'You can't do this! It's not fair!'

Fidelma rolled her eyes. '*MAM!*'

'Shh!' I hissed, glancing at Wilbert. But the noise had already woken him, and he was stretching like he was ready to begin a new day. I groaned as he bounded happily out of the room just before Debra looked in with a sympathetic smile.

'Sorry about this, Martin. But Fidelma has a lot of work to do and she needs to vary her study spaces. You can't expect her to just sit at the same desk all the time.'

'I'm not a robot, Martin,' said Fidelma.

'She's not a robot, love,' agreed their mother.

'I know she's not a robot!' snapped Martin. 'A robot wouldn't kick me out of my room! I wish she *was* a robot!'

'You should be proud,' his mother told him. 'Some day your sister's going to be the first female Taoiseach* of Ireland.'

***TAOISEACH** - pronounced 'tea-shook', as the first prime minister of Ireland always wanted his tea shaken, not stirred.

Martin shook his head at this terrifying thought and trudged away in defeat to the kitchen.

I let Wilbert outside to relieve himself, and we sat down at the table to resume our brainstorming session, but we were soon interrupted by Sister Number Two.

Trisha started digging through cupboards, banging pots and pans, and holding them up to her ears. She was trying to make a follow-up to her nose-ring design and was struggling to find an idea.

'All of this stuff is so boring!' she snapped. 'I need inspiration!'

'Maybe you should take a nice, long walk,' suggested Martin hopefully.

But he only succeeded in catching her attention.

'Gimme your shoes. I want to try them on as earrings.'

Martin had already lost his bedroom and wasn't about to lose his shoes too.

'Have you looked through the bin yet?' he asked. '*One man's garbage is another man's treasure!*'

Trisha turned to the smelly, overflowing bin. 'That's actually not a terrible idea . . .'

Moments later, she was rifling through the rubbish, and we tiptoed away as she tried to hook an empty egg box to her ear lobe.

Next, we tried the shed, but behind this door we found Sister Number Three. Sinead was savagely punching a sack of potatoes that was hanging before her like an Irish piñata*. Liam was helping her train for the Sack-Punching Finals, where she was due to face the Champion of South Roscommon, Fury O'Hare, a florist from the town of Knockcroghery. He roared encouragement as she pummelled the potatoes. 'C'mon, Sinead! No mercy! Slap those spuds!'

We backed away, and finally ended up on our favourite old spot – sitting on the back wall beneath the night sky. But we were too tired to brainstorm about N.P. any more, so we just watched Wilbert scamper around on the roof, howling at the moon.

'You know, Sean,' Martin mused dreamily, 'I can't wait till I'm an inventor and I've got my face on that Winners Wall with my Invention Convention trophy.'

***PIÑATA** - a Mexican punching bag filled with sweets. With their hot chilies, Mexicans love to give their food a bit of *kick*, so it makes sense that they also like to give their dessert a bit of *punch*.

'That's gonna be pretty sweet all right,' I agreed. 'But first, I presume we'll have to invent an invention – right?'

'Ah, that shouldn't be a problem. I've got ideas coming out the wazoo! And besides, I won't have to do it alone.'

'That's true – you'll have your trusty IF at your side!'

'Not just you, Sean,' he said, pulling out the application form. 'It says I can apply as a *team*, with up to three others.'

'A team of inventors?' I gasped. 'Martin, it's what you've always wanted!'

'Well – what I've always wanted is an army of trained monkeys. But I'm definitely getting closer!'

'So who are you going to recruit?'

'I'm not sure yet,' he said. 'But I want to win this thing, Sean. So I'm going to need the best of the best in Team Martin!'

CHAPTER NINE
TEAM MARTIN

That night, I didn't quite get my full forty winks of sleep – in fact, I barely got two or three winks, as the Wonkey refused to snooze. I read stories, rubbed his belly, hugged his hoofs, whistled up his nose, and everything else they suggested in the handbook, but it wasn't until Martin bounded out of bed, ready to start a new day, that Wilbert finally nodded off.

So I was feeling a little groggy as I sat at the back of the classroom listening to Mr Jackson drone on. But Martin was wide awake, eagerly putting his plan into motion. And as their teacher handed out results of a class test about what they did on their science trip, the determined boy took note of which students did best.

Alan	D+
Other Alan	Had chicken pox so did not attend.
Trevor	B
Paul	Cat ate homework.
Marco	D–
Conor Bonner	E+
Jonner Bonner	E+ – Accused of cheating from a failing student. His brother confirmed allegation.
John Joe	C+
Dicky	Caught chicken pox from other Ala

'Next up – Declan Mannion,' called Mr Jackson from the front of the room.

As Declan went up to retrieve his results, there were snickers from the rest of the class. This did not usually go too well.

'What's the damage, Jermaine?' Declan asked.

His teacher frowned at him, handing him back the test.

'F minus. We may as well get married, Declan – looks like we'll be spending the rest of our lives together in this classroom.'

There was a chuckle from the room. This soon died when Declan turned around and glared.

'No thanks, Jermaine. I'm never getting married again, but cheers for the offer.'

Declan walked off, leaving his teacher a little confused. Martin wrote down the latest poor result in his copybook.

'It's pretty slim pickings here, buddy,' I whispered.

'Yeah, when did kids get so dumb?'

'Trevor's got the best score so far.'

'He always does fairly well in tests. And don't his new glasses make him look particularly clever?'

'And so grown up,' I agreed.

'I should probably include him in the team – he loves being part of stuff.'

'Ah, yeah. It'll really make his day.'

The boy nodded, happy to be doing Trevor a huge favour.

'Trev . . .' Martin called, in a hushed but excited tone. 'Wanna be in a super-secret science team?'

'Yeah, whatever,' Trevor replied, barely looking up.

'Cool. Love the new glasses, by the way.'

'Thanks – they're my auntie's. Dad sat on mine.'

Martin turned back to me and I gave him an encouraging look. 'OK, so there's you. And there's Trevor. We're halfway there.'

But as Martin looked around the room, his confidence drained from his already pale face. Was there anyone else with the Right Stuff to be on Team Martin . . . ?

During break-time, we were cornered by an irate Padraic behind the bike sheds. He'd heard about Martin's plan and was shocked not to be automatically included.

'But you've got to have *me* in the group,' Padraic insisted. 'What kind of party doesn't invite the P-Dog?'

'Like I said before, Padraic, it's not a party.'

'Not without me it's not.'

'I'll tell you what, P, why don't you use this opportunity to sell yourself to me?'

'How much? I'll not take less than a fiver.'

'No, I mean, tell me what you'd bring to Team Martin.'

'Well,' Padraic said. 'A better flippin' name for a start.'

'C'mon, P!'

'OK, OK. Well . . . I'm punctual.'

'I can't argue with that; you're a wonderful timekeeper.'

'I always carry a spare sandwich in my pocket,' added Padraic, pulling out a soggy sarnie from his trousers.

'Noted,' Martin noted.

'I'm good with animals.'

'Not sure how that'll help, but OK.'

'I'm excellent at maths.'

'That one is *not* true.'

'Nope, that one was a lie – I'll admit to that.'

'I dunno, Padraic. I really need the best of the best!'

'I put the A in team!' Padraic exclaimed, holding up his science results.

'Did you get an A in the test?' Martin asked, surprised.

'No, I got a C minus.'

'Well, there's no C in team, Padraic.'

'There's a C in cream. Can I be in some cream?'

'I want to win this thing, P, and I need every team member to bring something special.'

'OK, well, what you'll get from me is total loyalty. One hundred and ten per cent. Loyalty, plus the aforementioned spare sandwich.'

Martin considered his friend's plea.

'P-Dog – you know I can't say no to a sandwich. You're in!'

'In what?' came a voice behind us.

We turned to find Declan Mannion staring at us, with a cigar in his mouth. He was certainly not part of the plan.

'In, eh . . .' Martin tried to think quickly of something. 'In . . . school. I was just telling Padraic that he's in school. He was saying that this was a hospital, and I was assuring him that he's not having surgery today. Because he's in school.'

'Good save, buddy,' I lied.

'In what?' Declan repeated, this time looking at Padraic.

'We're all in a big party!' Padraic replied excitedly.

'It's not a flippin' party!' Martin hissed.

Declan noticed the entry form in Martin's hand and snatched it from his feeble grasp.

'What the flip is an Invention Convention?' he demanded.

'Oh, it's just some boring classwork-based nonsense. It's certainly not the kind of thing you'd be—'

'The winners get gold medals?' Declan noted, still reading the entry form. 'Grand, I'm in too.'

'What? But . . . I don't think you'll enjoy it, Dec—'

'I need gold. I don't trust paper money any more. All my operations are moving to gold.'

Martin looked to me. I shrugged. I've always liked Declan. He's the kind of guy that's good to know. In prison.

'Cool,' Martin lied. 'I'll let you know the details when I—'

But Declan had already walked off. He was in.

'*Now* it's a party!' Padraic added, before skipping off to the toilets.

Martin considered the newly formed team. He seemed less than impressed with what he'd just created.

'Sean, I bet those kids from St Whimmion's are as sharp as a Wonkey's front teeth. What have *we* got?'

I looked out at Padraic skipping happily away with a party in his step, Trevor poorly bouncing a basketball in his auntie's reading glasses, and Declan 'Can't-Stop-Failing-Sixth-Class' Mannion playing blackjack on a beer keg.

'It's not just about brains, Martin. Finding the right mix is the key to a successful team,' I told him confidently.

'I don't know, Sean . . .'

'Look at the A Team*. They've got a wily** old con man – for us, that's Declan. They've got the handsome charmer with a twinkle in his eye – that's Trevor.'

***THE A TEAM** - an underground crime-fighting force. Their mysterious endeavours were compromised when a documentary was made about them and broadcast on television throughout the 1980s and 1990s. They were then easily found and arrested by two policemen who watched the show.

****WILY** - shrewd, astute and especially deceitful. Originally named after a gentleman named Willy, who was as canny as a fox, but a terrible speller.

'Yeah,' Martin agreed. 'Those new glasses do make his dull eyes sparkle.'

'They've got the tough guy who's afraid of aeroplanes.'

'I did once see Padraic duck under a table when he saw someone making a paper jet,' Martin agreed.

'And lastly, they've got the crazy loon.' As I pointed at Martin, he seemed unimpressed by his status in the group.

'The crazy loon?'

'The wild card,' I assured him. 'The man of mystery who always surprises the enemy.'

'Well, I do surprise myself many times daily,' he agreed. 'You're right, Sean. We can do this!'

'We sure can, kiddo. All we need now is a better name.'

'Hmmm,' Martin thought. 'How about The A-Team?'

'I feel like that one's kinda taken, buddy.'

'The B-Team?'

'The B-Team? Hmmm. I like it! I like it a lot.'

'Agreed, Sean!' he cried. 'What sounds more like victory than The B-Team?!'

CHAPTER TEN
THE BIG IDEA

A few days later, Declan ordered the boys to come over to his house after school for their first team meeting. I'd hoped to bring Wilbert along too, but Martin didn't want any mayhem at the Mannion home, so Crunchie Wonkey-sat for me. By which I mean, the Wonkey sat on top of him and nodded off.

I felt bad that I wasn't spending more quality time with Wilbert, but I was busy IFing for Martin, and whenever I had a spare moment I was trying to solve the mystery of the N.P. – without much luck. However, I was still determined to be the greatest pet owner a Wonkey could ever wish for, so I vowed to comb him, cuddle him, and maybe even milk him that very evening – right after our science session at the Mannion lair.

None of the boys had been to Declan's house before. In fact, Martin was surprised to hear that Declan even lived in a house. Surely no normal home was wild enough or dangerous enough to house the enigmatic Declan Mannion! Martin had assumed that Declan simply drove a truck around all night, puffing on cigars and betting on late-night badger races.

But surprisingly enough, it seemed that there was an actual Mannion home. And when we arrived at its gate, along with Padraic and Trevor, we were all astonished. It was a very normal-looking house, with a red door and some pretty rose bushes in the front garden.

'This is actually quite pleasant!' said Martin admiringly, as we strode confidently through the gate.

'A lovely, fragrant home,' agreed Padraic, sniffing the roses.

But then came the dogs.

Oh holy moly. The dogs.

The gate had barely clicked shut behind them when they came galloping around the side of the house. Fourteen of them, I counted! All greyhounds. The fastest dogs on the planet.

'Arghhhhh!' screamed the boys, sprinting away.

Around the house they all went, in a shrieking, barking blur of dark fur, snapping teeth and sweaty, terrified faces. Around and around they raced. It was one of those times I was quite relieved to be a figment of Martin's imagination, and I leaned against the gatepost lazily, watching the pursuit.

Finally Declan appeared at the front door. 'Stop bothering me pups!' he barked.

'Sorry – (*gasp!*) – Declan!' panted Padraic, as they hoofed it across the front garden.

'You're getting them all sweaty!' complained Declan.

Moments later, the tormented trio reappeared at the other side of the house and ran past Declan again. Martin called, 'Hey, Declan, is there . . .'

On their third lap around him, he continued: '. . . any chance you . . .'

Fourth lap: '. . . could ask them to . . .'

Fifth lap: '. . . stop chasing us, please?!'

Sixth lap: Declan looked confused. 'What was that, Moone?'

'Call 'em off!' screamed Trevor.

Declan shrugged and made various loud grunts, tongue-clicks and whistles that stopped the dogs in their tracks.

'Yup. Heagh! Dow'boy. G'wan! Hup now!'

It sounded like he was speaking a different language, but suddenly the dogs were all wagging their tails and nuzzling Declan happily. He was a skilled pet owner, I had to give him that.

'Aren't they beauties?' he called.

'Oh gorgeous, gorgeous,' muttered Padraic, who was drenched with sweat.

'A good s-s-spring in their step,' stammered Trevor, who was visibly shaking.

'Very healthy-looking teeth,' wheezed Martin, who noticed that the bottom of his trouser leg had been chewed off.

'I'm breeding them!' explained Declan proudly. 'One of my many side-businesses. They're gonna make me a fortune. Just like you science lads. You're my new pups!' He chuckled, and then gestured towards the house. 'Hup now! In with ye! G'wan!'

The lads didn't wait to be asked twice, and we all hoofed it into the house. It was a relief to escape the dogs, but once in the hallway they were attacked again – this time by a horde of hares*!

'I'm breeding hares too!' explained Declan, as Martin got kicked in the face by one of those long-eared lunatics. 'Ya can't have greyhounds without hares!'

Eventually the team got settled on a couch in an animal-free room, and Declan surveyed them from his throne-like armchair. 'Well then,' he began. 'Have ye got my gold yet?'

The boys looked at each other.

'Eh. Not yet, Mr Mannion,' admitted Martin. 'First, we need to complete the application

***HARES** – sworn enemies of greyhounds. Cousins of rabbits, but larger and faster, unless they're racing a tortoise, which tends to make them overconfident and sleepy.

form. There's just a few minor details left.'

'Such as?'

'Our team name. I've taken the liberty of calling us "The B-Team". That OK? I've already pencilled it in.'

'Well, then you can pencil it back out again, Moone,' said Declan.

I was gobsmacked. 'He doesn't like it? "The B-Team" is a brilliant name! It took us ages to come up with that!'

'Any other suggestions?' asked Declan, throwing it out to the group.

'How about . . . the Science Squad?' suggested Padraic excitedly.

'Or the Big Bangers of Boyle?' called out Trevor.

'The Inventor Tormentors!' came another suggestion.

'The Roscommon Radioactives!'

'The Tremendous Trevors!'

'The Mengineers!'

'Team Martin?'

'Those names are all rubbish!' snapped Declan dismissively. 'We need something amazing that tells the world that we're the most incredible inventors ever!'

The boys nodded, and then sat in silence.

'How about we put *bits* of our names together to form a *new* name?' offered Trevor.

They looked at him blankly.

'Like this,' he said, pulling out a piece of paper. He wrote down their four names and then circled various letters.

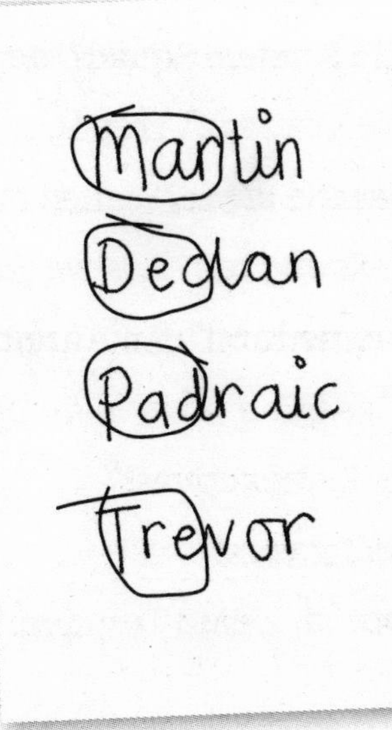

'Mar . . . Dec, Pad . . . Tre,' murmured Trevor.

'Mardec Padtre. That's genius!' exclaimed Padraic. 'It's like you're using science to come up with our science name!'

Trevor circled more letters. 'Or . . . Trevartin Decraic?'

'Trevartin Decraic! Even better!'

'We're definitely getting closer,' agreed Declan.

'Are we though?' I asked, less convinced.

'Or how about this one?' Trevor went on. 'Tre . . . P . . . De . . . M?'

Declan stood up. 'Trepdem! That's the one! That's our name! We are Team Trepdem!' he roared, and punched the air.

Martin seemed less excited. 'Are we sure it doesn't sound like some kind of . . . disease?' he asked. 'Like . . . *I've got a nasty dose of Trepdem?*'

There was a pause.

Then Declan shouted, 'Team Trepdem! Hear us roar!'

Padraic, Trevor and Declan all roared passionately.

Martin and I rolled our eyes – we were clearly outvoted.

'Trepdem it is.' He sighed, and added it to the form.

They moved on to the second task, which was a description of their invention. This proved to be more challenging.

It seemed that coming up with something ingenious wasn't quite as easy as they'd hoped, so Martin suggested that they just fill out the form with some nonsense to avoid missing the deadline, and they could worry about the big idea later.

'But how can we explain our idea without . . . explaining our idea?' asked Padraic.

Martin got up and started to pace around.

'Don't hold back, buddy,' I told him. 'You've gotta make this sound as exciting as possible – while also saying absolutely nothing.'

Martin nodded and turned back to his team-mates.

'We cannot reveal too much about our invention right now . . .' he began.

Trevor grabbed a pen and started writing this on to the form.

'But know this!' Martin went on. *'It will defy the laws of gravity, the laws of physics, and most of the laws of Ireland. We all know what the world's greatest inventions are . . .'*

'The Toaster?' I suggested.

'The Toaster! The Toasted-Cheese-Sandwich Maker! And . . .'

'You can't enjoy toasties without a cup of tea,' I reminded him.

'The Kettle!' he cried. *'But if you were to multiply them each by a thousand, you'd still be nowhere near the amazingness of our invention! Science will not know what hit it! And if you grant us a place in the Invention Convention, we will share our mind-blowing*

miracle with you and the world! DO IT, SCIENCE PEOPLE! IF YOU DARE!'

The lads applauded, mightily impressed.

'Right, then there's the issue of the entry fee,' noted Trevor.

Declan pulled out a roll of banknotes from his sock. He peeled off a few twenties and tossed them at Trevor. 'Gotta spend money to make money!'

'Great stuff!' chirped Trevor. 'So all we need now is the signature of our teacher, to prove that everything we're saying about our invention is true.'

'But none of it's true,' pointed out Martin.

'How are we going to get Mr Jackson to sign?' worried Padraic.

But Declan calmly reached out for the form. 'Gentlemen. Allow me.'

He took a pen and forged the signature of their teacher with great ease, as if he'd done it many, many times before.

FOR OFFICE USE ONLY

✂ . . . .

Section 8: Teacher's Declaration.

I hereby agree to supervise the work of Team Treptem and will make sure that they always behave in a safe, responsible and science-friendly manner and will never cause explosions, ignite electromagnetic storms, open intergalactic wormholes, burn carpets or frighten cats.

I confirm that their invention will be designed and built by the students alone, with no help from me or anybody else.

I also acknowledge that if there are any lies in this form, or shenanigans in general, I will pay a £10,000 fine and serve a short but deeply unpleasant term in jail.

Signed,

Mr Jermaine Jackson

CHAPTER ELEVEN
ROUND ONE

After all the Team Trepdem excitement, Martin and I were planning to have a nice, quiet evening at home. Martin fancied a bath to calm his nerves after his escape from Declan's dogs, and I was hoping to spend some quality time with Wilbert.

When I collected him from an exhausted and dishevelled Crunchie, I borrowed a couple of books from my wrestler pal called *Mysteries of the Imaginary World* and *A History of Weird Bottles*, which I hoped might shed some light on the N.P. puzzle. Crunchie wasn't much of a reader, but kept a large collection of books to pad the walls of his 'home wrestling studio' (his kitchen).

But before I could turn to N.P.-solving, there

was a Wonkey to milk. And although those weird little things on his belly kinda freaked me out, the handbook assured me that Wonkey-milking was a delightful bonding experience for both IF and IP (Imaginary Pet).

'But I thought you'd already bonded,' said Martin as we walked up the Moone driveway. 'Didn't I see him hugging you yesterday?'

'Actually, I think the little scamp was trying to strangle me with his hoofs!' I chuckled. 'But I'm sure that once we have a nice milking session, we'll be the best of buds. Duck, Martin!' I yelled, as some pink pellets came flying over our heads, just missing us.

'Sorry about that. He keeps throwing his poop at me. *Bad Wilbert, bad!*' I scolded. But the Wonkey just honked with laughter.

When Martin opened the front door, he found his family gathered in the hallway, waiting for him, and his bath plans quickly disappeared down the plughole.

'Ah, there ya are, Martin!' exclaimed his mother. 'Quick – into the car.'

'Where are we going?'

'Where do you think?' replied his dad, who was wearing a white T-shirt with the words 'Up, Sinead!' scrawled on it in black marker. 'Sinead's got her big sack-punch tonight. The county final!'

'It's the best out of three,' added Debra excitedly, 'so if she wins tonight, she'll be halfway to the crown of Roscommon!'

Fidelma sighed, wearing a T-shirt that read 'No Mercy, Moone'. 'Are we ready yet? I've tons of studying to do.'

'Trisha!' hollered Liam towards the girls' bedroom.

Finally she appeared, wearing potato earrings, with the words 'Sack her good, Sinead!' scrawled across her face in red lipstick. It looked slightly scary, but Liam ignored that fact since it was also quite supportive.

'Right, everyone in the car! And no one talk to Sinead,' warned Liam. 'She's in the zone!'

As they piled into the car, Martin whispered to me, 'You stay here, Sean, and after you milk Wilbert, work on the N.P. mystery. That's a lot more important than watching Sinead punch potatoes.'

'Will do,' I promised. 'But fill me in later!'

Martin gave a salute and squeezed into the back seat beside Sinead, who was meditating.

'Hi, Sinead!' he chirped.

She immediately punched him, giving him a perfect dead arm without even opening her eyes.

'Ow!'

'I said no talking, Martin! Don't let him distract you, Sinead!' Liam called as he started the engine. 'Stay in the zone! Just stay in the zone!'

He floored the accelerator, and they sped away.

*

A little later, the Moones were seated near the stage in the packed Roscommon Town Hall, waiting for the two sack warriors to appear.

'Looks like Sinead's the favourite to win!' exclaimed Debra as she glanced over at the bookies*, who were taking the final bets. 'Should we put some money on her?'

'Don't worry, love, I've already bet Martin's entire college fund,' Liam informed her.

'You've what?!' blurted Martin.

'Relax, Martin – it was only twenty quid,' admitted his dad.

'Let's get ready to rummmmbbbbllllle!' came a voice from the stage. They looked up to see a priest in his black outfit, who was also

BOOKIE** – short for 'bookmaker', even though they don't actually make books, as I discovered when I asked one to make ***The Blunder Years. Instead I ended up betting on a horse called 'Only A Big Eejit Would Bet On Me', which I thought was just a funny name, but turned out to be amazingly accurate.

wearing a red sparkly jacket that would have looked more at home in Las Vegas. 'Haha, always wanted to do that. Welcome to the Roscommon Final of the World Sack-Punching Championships!'

The crowd roared and pounded their feet with excitement.

'This event really puts the *fun* into *fun*draiser, and the cha-*ching* into sack-pun*ching*!' joked the priest into the mic. 'Thanks to all of you, we've raised enough money to put that new roof on the church toilet – and that's what really matters tonight, isn't it? That's why we're *really* here.'

There was a confused smattering of applause.

'Only joking!' chuckled the priest. 'We're here for sack-punching – am I right?'

The crowd erupted into cheers.

'Hahaha. Lovely stuff. Then let's bring out the contenders! In the red corner, all the way from beautiful Boyle, she's a freestyle sack-puncher!

She's a biter, she's a kicker, she doesn't care what she does so long as she gets the job done. She's the Majestic Moone, Sinead the Scrapper! Give it up for the Champion of North Roscommon . . . Sinead Moone!'

There was a mighty roar as Sinead wandered out in her tracksuit and stood on stage looking bored as the audience chanted her name.

'Moone! Moone! Moone!'

'And in the blue corner,' the priest continued, 'from rocky Knockcroghery, we have the light-footed florist, the dancing gardener, the titan with the trowel. She smells like petals and has fists like metal, it's the Champion of South Roscommon . . . Fury O'Hare!'

Another cheer, and out came Mrs O'Hare. She was a small, kind-faced lady in her sixties, and was still wearing her florist's apron with the name of her shop on it: 'Let's Talk Some Scents'.

She waved at the crowd, and then glared at Sinead icily.

'Lower the sacks!' shouted the priest.

From the rafters, two sacks of potatoes were lowered on ropes – one for each contender.

'Each sack holds three hundred medium-sized potatoes,' continued the priest, 'thoroughly washed, with skin still on. There's only one rule here, folks: punch until mashed. Whoever pulverizes every potato first will win tonight's battle. And whoever wins two battles will take the sack-punching crown of Roscommon. Fighters, are we ready?'

Fury O'Hare took off her wedding ring and popped it in her apron pocket. Sinead spat out her chewing gum.

The crowd waited with bated breath.

'But first,' shouted the priest, 'let's have a quick prayer.'

He bowed his head. A few members of the confused audience lowered their heads too and started muttering a Hail Mary.

'Only joking!' chuckled the priest. 'Let's SACK-PUNCH!!!'

A bell rang out, and the battle began.

*

Back at home, I was feeding Wilbert a saucer of chopped onions, and while he gobbled them up, I reread the chapter on milking techniques.

How to Milk Your Wonkey in Six Easy Steps

1. Play some soothing music.
2. Light some candles.
3. Make sure your hands are warm.
4. Grasp the Wonkey's udder, and squish gently, but firmly, like squeezing a tiny roll of toothpaste.
5. Sing to your Wonkey as you fill your milk jug.
6. Afterwards, tickle your Wonkey's ears and offer it an ice-cream cake.

Music: check.

Candles: check.

Warm hands: check.

But things started to go wrong at Number 4. I grasped his little udder as firmly and gently as I could, but he didn't like that one bit, and whacked me across the face with a hoof.

'Wilbert!' I cried. 'You need to be milked—'

Whack!

'– once a month or your milk—'

Whack!

'– will turn to cheese and you'll get cheese cramps!'

Whack! Whack! Whack!

He stood up on his hind legs and jiggled his belly, trying to shake me off, but I clung on tighter. Then he spun me around in circles. As I whirled around him, I used my free hand to see if the handbook had any other suggestions.

It read: '*If your Wonkey is reluctant to be milked, then cradle it in your arms and sprinkle kisses on its nose.*'

Just then, I lost my grip with my udder hand and went crashing across the room.

Wilbert brayed with laughter as I struggled to my feet and staggered towards him in a daze. When I stooped down to pick him up and cradle him, he simply sat down on top of me.

And there he stayed – no matter how much I struggled and shrieked.

I lay on the floor with a face full of buttock, and began to wonder if I was really cut out to be a Wonkey-owner.

'So much for *quality* time,' I sighed sadly, 'And so much for solving the mystery of N.P . . .'

Meanwhile, in the hall, the battle was still raging.

'C'mon, Sinead!' shouted Debra. 'Mash those spuds!'

'Slap that sack, Sinead!' bellowed Liam. 'Slap it like it's your worst enemy!'

'Yeah, slap it like it's me!' suggested Martin.

But it was clear to them all that Sinead

was struggling. She was exhausted, and her punch-rhythm was slowing down. It was understandable of course – she'd been whacking a sack of potatoes for twenty-six minutes – but Fury O'Hare seemed, if anything, to be getting faster. As Sinead slowed, there was a new spring in the florist's step, sensing victory.

Fury's tiny fists were a blur. She danced around her sack, landing left and right hooks as fast as lightning, floating like a butterfly and slicing like a butter knife.

'C'mon, Sinead!' urged Liam desperately.

But a few precise punches later, the little old lady obliterated the last spuds in her sack and raised her small red fists in victory as the final bell rang out.

Back in the car, the Moones drove home in silence, trying to come to terms with the shocking loss of Round One.

'You were robbed, Sinead!' said Liam suddenly. 'Robbed!'

Debra nodded bitterly. 'That woman's potatoes must have been parboiled*!'

But Sinead just shrugged. 'Fury fought a good fight. I lost fair and square.'

'Well, it's not over yet,' Liam reminded her. 'It's the best out of three, so you've got one more chance to beat her. Right, Sinead?'

But Sinead just stared out the window.

In some ways, Martin was glad that there was one less winner in the house lording it over him, but he also felt sorry for his sister. He knew that losing wasn't pleasant, and it was something that he really wanted to avoid with this science adventure. He couldn't bear the thought of those posh kids from St Whimmion's laughing at him or his friends again, and putting their

***PARBOILED** – a cooking term meaning 'part-boiled'. There's no 't' because cooks use fewer letters depending on how boiled it is. 'Parbled' = more than half. 'Pbled' = very well boiled. 'Ble' = mush.

rich, dirtless hands all over those shiny science medals.

Martin wanted to win this time. And Sinead's defeat made him hope even more desperately that their application would be successful, so they could take gold at the Invention Convention. His face could only take its rightful place on the Winners Wall if they won. There was no 'Runners-Up Wall', or 'You Tried Your Best Wall', or 'Your Mammy Bought You A Medal And Told Us To Give It To You Wall'. Not this time.

Winning was crucial, Martin decided. Winning was vital. Winning was the most important thing ever.

CHAPTER TWELVE
EXPERIMENTS

The next morning, I let Wilbert loose in the field next door and dived into the task of solving the mystery of N.P.

My head was swirling with questions:

1. What did it mean?
2. What were those crispy bits I ate?
3. How was I going to solve this?
4. Should I eat a sandwich first?

It was quite the pickle. I needed some answers. And a sandwich. And maybe a pickle. But mostly answers.

I devoured Crunchie's books (not literally, as I'd already devoured a sandwich and a pickle), but found them to be quite useless – not a single mention of 'N.P.'

However, if books have taught me anything, it's that the best place to find answers is in a book. Although I suppose books *would* say that. But if you think about it, the only place *you're* going to find the answer to the N.P. mystery is *in this book.* So maybe they're right!

Either way, during my downtime – when Martin was asleep or having a sudsy bath, and Wilbert was having a long, leisurely bum-scratch – I started popping back to the imaginary world to scour the books in the 'Imaginary Research Facility For IFs Trying To Solve Weird Mysteries, Unexplained Anomalies And Wordsearch Puzzles With Their Realsies'. Or the I.R.F.F.I.T.T.S. W.M.U.A.A.W.P.W.T.R. for short.

One week later, I was still no closer to solving the mystery – but when Martin returned home from school one day, we did finally get *one* answer. There was a letter waiting for him in a shiny gold envelope stamped with the official seal of the Invention Convention!

The Invention Convention
Dublin, Ireland

Greetings, Team Trepdem!

Thank you for your application. I daresay we have never received a proposal before that told us so little about an invention. In fact, you told us literally nothing, except that 'Science will not know what hit it'. As scientists ourselves, I can assure you that we always know what hits it.

However, we were also intrigued by your impressive claims. And since your teacher, Mr Jackson, has signed your form and therefore vouched for your work (at risk of a massive fine and short jail sentence), we must assume that your invention is indeed a thousand times better than the toaster, the toasted-cheese-sandwich maker and the kettle all combined. This is a very exciting prospect indeed!

Therefore it is our great honour to invite you to participate in this year's Invention Convention!

Congratulations, Team Trepdem!

Please transport your invention to the Convention Centre in Dublin by noon on the 20th of June for judging. After the winners are announced, there will be a short dance party. This will be followed by tea and buns. Tea is free, buns are extra.

All the best,

Mrs Maggie Magoonty
(Top Science Judge)

*

'We're in?!' gasped Padraic, when Martin showed the letter to the gang the next day at school.

Declan Mannion was pleased. 'Guess I won't have to make any anonymous threatening phone calls after all. That's my weekend freed up.'

'So what happens now?' asked Trevor.

Martin gave him a determined look. 'Now we get to work!'

And get to work they did.

While I continued to trawl through the I.R.F.F. I.T.T.S.W.M.U.A.A.W.P.W.T.R., poring over every book with either an 'N' or a 'P' in the title, Team Trepdem constructed their first invention: a pair of rocket boots.

This might sound a bit dangerous, but what the team lacked in knowledge, they made up for in grit, enthusiasm and a total disregard for health and safety.

The rocket boots consisted of two big mucky boots, which came from Padraic's farm – their main test site. The second ingredient was fireworks. Declan bought the largest available from Boyle's black-market dealers (the Bonner brothers). The third and final ingredient was some strong, sticky tape. And once these three ingredients were combined – which took about forty-six seconds – they just needed a volunteer.

Everyone wanted to be the first rocketeer, but after an epic coin-flipping tournament, it was Trevor who claimed the lucky spot.

Invention 1: Rocket Boots

He pulled on the flight footwear eagerly, imagining himself soaring over the treetops like a boot-wearing budgie, and it was only after they'd lit the fuses that a thought suddenly occurred to Martin.

'Hang on . . . Don't fireworks explode?' he asked.

Trevor's face went pale just before his feet flew out from underneath him. He slammed on to his back, and was then dragged along the ground by his fiery boots.

Within seconds, he was at the far side of Padraic's field, screaming all the way, and would surely have had his feet melted, had the fizzing fireworks not carried him directly into a pond. They were extinguished in the water before they could pop, and instead of being exploded, Trevor merely found himself in a fight with a duck.

Now, it should be said that all inventors have setbacks. Harry Ferguson's tractors fizzled, sputtered, collapsed and crumpled before they hummed like Lamborghinis*. He crashed his home-made tractors, motorbikes, aeroplanes and racing cars countless times. Failed experiments came with the territory. But after the near-demise of Trevor, the team decided to make three Safety Rules.

1. Avoid fire.
2. Avoid ducks.
3. Avoid death.

Hoping to steer clear of these hazards for their second invention, they decided to try something simpler: a Coat Zipperer.

At least, the *idea* was simpler, but the same couldn't be said for the actual invention. It

***LAMBORGHINI** - the Cristiano Ronaldo** of cars. Fast, shiny, expensive, and a little bit ridiculous.

****CRISTIANO RONALDO** - the SUV*** of soccer players. Reliable, with a spectacular boot, but tends to tip over a lot.

*****SUV** - oh, just google it, ya lazybones!

consisted of a metal belt that was worn around the waist. This held a long rod that arched up from the lower back and over the wearer's head like a big 'C'. A spring-loaded hook dangled down from this towards the front of the coat where it could be attached to the zipper. By pulling two levers, the spring-loaded hook would pop up, taking the zipper with it, and – hey presto! – you were zipped and ready to go!

That was the idea, anyway, and since Padraic was the one who came up with it, it was decided that he should be the one to test it out. He put on his coat, and then the rest of the team helped him strap on the heavy Coat Zipperer. Soon the hook was attached to the zipper, the spring was primed, and all was ready.

Padraic held the levers.

'Activating zip!'

'Activating zip!' repeated Martin, with a nod.

Padraic hesitated nervously. 'Eh. In T-minus three, two, one . . .'

Finally he pulled the levers. 'Zip away!'

Nothing happened.

He pulled again. 'Zip away!'

Still nothing. Padraic leaned down towards the zip, peering at it, and pulled again.

Suddenly the spring popped, and the zip was yanked upward with such force that Padraic's whole head disappeared inside his coat. He gave a muffled wail, completely trapped.

Invention 2: The Coat Zipperer

Following these experiments, Padraic and Trevor strongly suggested that they build something that didn't need to be worn. So they decided to construct a robot.

Using scrap metal, some old bits of plastic and wood, they built an impressive-looking mechanical man, which they named the 'Trepdem Bot'.

But it had one slight flaw: it didn't actually

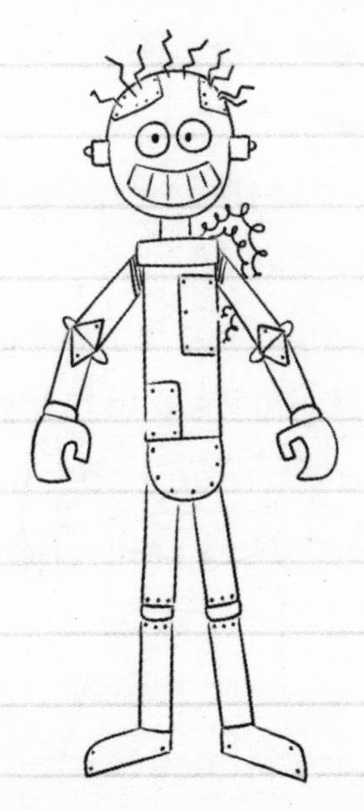

Invention 3: The Trepdem Bot

do anything. This was due to some confusion about who was in charge of electronics.

'I thought *you* were doing that, Trevor!' snapped Declan accusingly.

'No, I was in charge of hair. Padraic was in charge of electronics.'

'No, I was in charge of giving the robot a lovely smile!' insisted Padraic.

They all blamed each other and ended up with a robot that was completely hollow. It did nothing but stand there, like a big, smiling, futuristic failure.

As they stared at their mindless creation, Martin suddenly had an idea.

'Ya know, gang, if I've learned anything from films, it's that if you want to bring something to life, or go back in time, or become magnetic, or get any superpowers really, there's only one thing you need.'

'Batman?' suggested Padraic.

'*Lightning!*' proclaimed Martin. 'Lightning can do anything! That's science!'

'But this isn't like *Back to the Future**,' argued Trevor. 'How are we supposed to get our hands on some lightning? We don't know when it's going to strike.'

Declan spat on the ground. 'I know a fella that might be able to get us some. Wouldn't be cheap, though.'

They pondered this for a moment . . . when suddenly Padraic blurted, 'I've got it!'

'You've got lightning?' asked Martin.

'Nope. But we've got the next best thing at our farm. An electric fence!'

And so, forgetting about Safety Rule # 3 ('Avoid death'), they cycled out to Padraic's farm to electrocute their robot. Padraic didn't think that his dad, Farmer O'Dwyer, would approve of this experiment, so they decided to carry it out under cover of darkness.

***BACK TO THE FUTURE** – a film about time-travelling, setting roads on fire, and the dangers of kissing your mammy.

As the sun set, Team Trepdem waited patiently in the bushes until Mr and Mrs Farmer O'Dwyer were settled on the couch watching *Winning Streak**.

The four science ninjas then crept up to the electric fence with their robot. Padraic opened the control box and switched off the fence's power before Martin and Declan leaned the robot against the metal wires. The Trepdem Bot drooped backwards over the fence like a clumsy gymnast trying to do The Crab.

'Ready?' hissed Padraic.

'Ready!' Martin whispered back.

Padraic pressed a button, turning the fence back on, and then shoved a lever upward, jamming it up to full power.

There was a low, intense HUMMMMMMMMM, and the robot started to vibrate.

***WINNING STREAK** - an Irish TV game-show where the victor sprints around in the nude holding a giant cheque.

'Something's happening!' Martin squealed, astonished.

'Is it coming alive?' called Trevor, who was standing a very safe distance away.

'Yes! I think it's coming alive!' cried Martin.

The robot was starting to smoulder. Thick smoke began to billow out from underneath it. And then suddenly it burst into flames.

'Oh balls!' moaned Martin.

All four of them fled in a panic, running in different directions.

Behind them, there was a crackle from the fence, a pop from the control box – and then Padraic's house went dark. His neighbour's house went dark. And then every house in Boyle went dark, as the whole town was plunged into a blackout.

CHAPTER THIRTEEN
BARNEY BUNTON'S SECRET

Later that night, while the rest of the family stumbled around the house looking for torches and glow-in-the-dark T-shirts, Martin lay on his bed, feeling like he was being enveloped by the darkness of defeat. But then he lit a candle and felt better. Then he realized it was a scented candle, which Sinead had given him as a joke for Christmas, and he felt worse. But it turned out that the joke was on her, because that candle smelt flippin' divine! And with the fragrance of lilacs and orange peel wafting around him, he felt better than ever.

The thing about Martin Moone was that he never stayed down for long. He seemed to have an almost *elastic* rear end, and no matter how often he failed and floundered, he would always rebound, ready for more! It was simultaneously his best and worst characteristic. He never gave up. Even if it led to more failures, broken dreams and broken limbs – which it often did – he never threw in the towel.

However, when he thought about the team's recent disappointments – the robot ablaze on the electric fence, Trevor rocketing into a duck nest, and Padraic's mother trying to snip her son out of his coat – he fell into a funk* again.

When Realsies are at their low points, they need their IFs more than ever, so, thankfully, Wilbert and I tumbled out of the wardrobe at that very moment, on our way back from my latest research trip to the imaginary world.

'Martin, I've got it!' I cried excitedly.

He peered at the plastic baggy in my hand. 'Got what?'

'Oh . . . No, that's just Wilbert's poop. We were

***FUNK** – it can mean 'gloominess', a cool type of music, or a bad smell. So it's a bit like a sad, stinky slacker who plays guitar.

doing walkies.' I tossed the bag to Wilbert, and he caught it on his head. 'Bury that somewhere, will ya, pal?'

The Wonkey gave an annoyed 'Harrumph!', but trotted away, and I turned back to Martin. 'What I meant was, I've solved it! I've solved the mystery!'

'What mystery?'

'*N.P.*, of course!'

'Right! Sorry, I've been too busy trying to come up with inventions to think about that.'

'Well, I might just have a solution for your invention problem too,' I told him with a grin. Then I looked around, distracted. 'What is that smell? It's heavenly!'

'It's my scented candle! Isn't it incredible?'

We breathed it in for a while, and then I sat down beside him. 'So anyway. As you know, in the last couple of weeks, I've been spending a lot of time at the Imaginary Research Facility For IFs Trying To Solve Weird Mysteries—'

'You mean, the library?'

'Yes, it's basically just a big library,' I admitted. 'And I've had a breakthrough, Martin! I think I know what the N.P. on Barney Bunton's mysterious bottle might be.'

Martin nodded slowly. 'Is it Nun Pots?'

I frowned. 'What? No.'

'Nearly Plums?'

'They're definitely not plums.'

'Never Plums?'

'Well, yes. But, no . . .'

'Nacho Pudding?'

'OK, let's not start this again. Here's what I think *N.P.* really means.'

'Ninja Pickles?'

'*Notion Potion!*' I cried.

Martin paused. 'Notion . . . Potion?'

'Notion Potion,' I repeated.

'What's a Notion Potion?'

I grinned at him and paced around, barely able to contain my excitement.

'The Notion Potion, Martin, is a mythical drink from the imaginary world – a brain-boosting beverage. And when you drink it, it fills your head with notions and ideas. They say that just a few sips can transform a complete moron into a mastermind! A buffoon into a brainiac! A simpleton into a . . . brillianton!'

'Wow! And what would it do for someone like me?' asked Martin.

I paused, confused.

'. . . Who's *not* a simpleton?'

'Oh. Right!' I nodded. 'Eh. It would make you . . . even less of a simpleton!'

'So this stuff would give me ideas?' he asked keenly.

'Beyond your wildest dreams, Martin! With a few gulps, you'd be able to speak different languages, play musical instruments, concoct mathematical formulas, code computer viruses, follow recipes without burning anything and, most importantly . . . design mind-blowing inventions!'

Martin's eyes lit up. He was utterly gripped now. 'Would I be able to finish this Wordsearch?' he asked.

I glanced at the puzzle from *The Marvellous Activity Manual* that had remained stubbornly incomplete for months.

'Martin, you'd be able to *write* Wordsearches!'

'Well, let's not go mad, Sean. Who wants to write Wordsearches?'

'Good point,' I admitted. 'But the possibilities are endless. The Notion Potion could be the very thing that will help you win the Invention Convention and finally get your face on the Winners Wall!'

'That's what I'm talkin' about!' cheered Martin, and gave me a high-five. But then he paused. 'Hang on. This is an *imaginary* drink – right?'

'Right.'

'So how can an *imaginary drink* give me *real ideas?*'

I frowned. 'Aren't I an imaginary person giving you real ideas right now?'

Martin thought about this. 'Hmm. Indeed you are, Sean! Which means that this might actually work!' he concluded. 'So how do we get our hands on this Notion stuff?'

'Well . . . that's the question, buddy. In my research, I found several old stories about the Notion Potion. None of them said for sure where it can be found. But one of the legends mentioned a magical well in a distant and dodgy corner of the imaginary world – a well that is located somewhere near the peak of Mount Figment.'

'Hang on, Sean. You keep talking about stories and legends. Do we even know if this stuff exists?'

'It *must* exist, Martin,' I insisted.

'Why?'

'Because Barney Bunton had a bottle of it hidden in his cap!' I reminded him, pulling it out. 'What else could *N.P.* stand for?'

He opened his mouth to make more ridiculous suggestions.

'Don't!' I snapped, and he shut his gob again.

'Barney Bunton must have had a supply of the Notion Potion,' I continued, 'and maybe this was the source of inspiration for all of Harry Ferguson's ingenious inventions! Either the Mad Mechanic or his imaginary friend might have been guzzling this stuff. How else could Ferguson have come up with so many incredible ideas? Do you really think a normal human being could just sit down and *invent the tractor*?'

Martin pondered this. 'But what about those nasty crunchy bits we found in the bottle? You ate them and nothing happened.'

'I've been wondering about that too,' I admitted. 'That can't have been the proper potion. If those crispy bits were the remains of it, then the liquid must have gone bad. I mean, you can't leave stuff in bottles for decades and expect it to stay fresh! Remember last week when you covered your burger in that watery ketchup? Or when you drank the milk with the lumps in it?' I reminded him. 'Even the Notion Potion must have a best-before date.'

'Yeah, I should really start reading those,' said Martin. 'So it's a powerful, but possibly perishable*, magical drink. You know what that reminds me of? The Salmon of Knowledge!'

'The what?'

It turned out that Martin's grandad had once told him the old Irish story of the Salmon of Knowledge. It was about a fish who became highly intelligent after eating nine hazelnuts that contained all of the world's wisdom.

***PERISHABLE** – likely to go bad. Mouldy bad, not evil bad – although if you leave mayonnaise in the sun for long enough it'll eventually turn into a portal to the Underworld.

Apparently, wisdom was stored in nuts back then. A poet caught the clever fish after pursuing it for seven years. He told his servant, Fionn mac Cumhaill, to cook up the salmon, but warned him not to eat any of it. Fionn did as he was told, frying it up nicely for his boss. But when he gave it a poke to see if it was done, he burned his finger, so stuck it in his mouth to soothe it. And by sucking on that single drop of fish fat, Fionn mac Cumhaill gained all the knowledge of the world.

'Yes! It's exactly like the Salmon of Knowledge,' I agreed, 'except in a kind of smoothie-form. The Notion Potion is basically a drinkable Salmon of Knowledge.'

'Sounds perfect!' exclaimed Martin. He was really pumped now, excited that this concoction of cleverness might help him win the Invention Convention and get his face on the Winners Wall before EOPS. 'We need that N.P. as soon as possible!'

'And as your trusty IF, it's up to me to get it for you!' I replied valiantly. 'I request to go on a quest, Martin.'

'Eh. OK. What does that mean?'

'It means that I'll be away for a while, and you mustn't imagine me until I return.'

'Why not?'

'Because if you do, I'll pop back here and will have to start the quest all over again.'

'Oh.'

Martin didn't like the thought of being IF-less, but he liked the thought of being Potionless even less.

'How long will you be gone?'

'Not long, I hope. But I will not stop questing until I find it!'

Martin considered all this for a moment, but then at last gave a nod. 'Very well, Sean. Quest request granted!'

We high-fived eagerly, and Martin smiled, his spirits soaring again.

'Mystery solved, quest under way, and a candle that smells like angels. Everything's coming up Moone!'

CHAPTER FOURTEEN
THE QUEST

I woke at first light.

I had a long journey ahead, so I knew that I needed to get an early start. My quest would take me deep into the far corners of the imaginary world, and I was ready to face any foes or challenges or weird-looking creatures I encountered . . . just as soon as I had another quick doze.

I woke again at second or third light.

Wilbert was licking my face, and this time I was ready to embark on my adventure! I let the Wonkey outside to pee, pulled on my quest-vest, and sat down to lace up my voyage-boots when I decided to rest my eyes for an absolute maximum of five seconds.

At fourth or fifth light, I woke once more.

'Get up, Sean, get up!' I shouted at myself.

From under the covers, Martin gave a grunt that might have been 'Shurrup, Sean', and from his sister's bed Sinead gave a louder grunt that might have been 'Shurrup, Martin!'

It was a Saturday, which meant that no Moone would be stirring till eighteenth or nineteenth light. So I gathered my quest-gear, and as I gazed down at Martin, slack-jawed and drooling all over his pillow, I hoped that this wouldn't be the last time I saw his idiotic face.

'Goodbye, little man,' I whispered, and he farted quietly in his sleep.

Outside the Moone home, I looked over my supplies, making sure that I was quest-ready:

- Swiss Army Knife ☑
- Belgian Army fork ☑
- Climbing Rope ☑
- Skipping Rope ☑
- Tractor Beam ☑

1 Tin of baked beans ☑
54 Tins of jelly beans ☑

With everything in place, I hoisted my adventure-backpack on to my shoulders, straightened my explorer-hat, and was just adjusting my expedition-undies when that bonkers IF Loopy Lou rolled out of the hedge.

'Whoopsie!' he sang, as he tumbled across the grass. He hopped to his feet and cried, 'Loopy Lou in da house!'

Behind him, Crunchie Haystacks gave a sigh as he ambled up the driveway. 'Lou, why can't ya just walk through a gate like a normal IF?'

'What's up, guys?' I asked. 'What brings ye to Moone Manor?'

'We hear you're going on a quest,' replied Crunchie.

'You hear right,' I told him. 'In fact, I'm about to start questing right now.'

'Not without *us* you're notty nots!' said Lou.

I looked at them both and couldn't help but

smile. It seemed that loyalty didn't just come in Wonkeys. It also came in clowns and wrestlers too.

'Welcome aboard, lads! Did you tell your IFs not to imagine you?'

'Eh. Were we supposed to do that?' asked Crunchie blankly.

'Whoopsie!' apologized Lou.

'You're not going to last long on the quest if they imagine you back,' I told them.

'Well, they're not imagining us right now, so let's get a move on!' urged Crunchie.

Just then I heard a 'Meerrghhllll' and turned to see my other loyal pal gazing up at me with his big dopey eyes.

'What is it, Wilbert – you want to come too?' I asked. 'Well, why not?'

'I can think of lotty lots of reasons why notty nots,' muttered Lou, and Crunchie nodded in agreement.

But I ignored them, patting Wilbert on the head. 'You should be right at my side!

An IF's Best Friend – right?'

The Wonkey looked confused, and then pointed to his udder patch, which was bulging like a pudgy pot-belly.

I sighed, disappointed. 'Oh you just want to be milked?'

Wilbert nodded eagerly.

'Getting cheese cramps, are ya?'

Wilbert nodded again.

'Sorry, pal. I've been so busy with the N.P. that I haven't had a chance to try again. But if you come along, I'll milk you on the road,' I promised, and he wagged his tail gratefully. 'Now let us begin our quest! To Mount Figment!' I cried heroically, and led them off down the driveway.

At the gate, Crunchie paused. 'Wouldn't it be quicker if we just went through Martin's wardrobe?'

'Actually, yes. Let's do that,' I agreed, and we all trudged back to the house.

*

We hopped through the wardrobe, eager to cover as much ground as possible while our three Realsies slept. On the far side, we found ourselves in the town of Balderdash, where I quickly caught a cab (short for 'cabbage'). We gobbled it down and hurried to the tram station (trampoline station). One good bounce took us into the countryside, where we then found a Rick Shaw. Mr Shaw was an old friend of mine, and kindly lent us his giant turtle to complete our journey. It's basically the only safe mode of transport through the Swamp of Daydreams. Hector, the Piranha-Gator, is a nasty creature, but he knows better than to tangle with a giant, magical turtle with poisonous knees.

Finally we were on the road to Mount Figment, which was long and winding. Then it became short and straight. Then it was bright and bouncy for a bit. Then it got wet and wobbly. Then warm and chocolatey. Then scary, then silly. Then so silly it was scary.

Then it got a bit boring and I fell asleep. And then suddenly we were at the foot of Mount Figment!

'Whoa, Nelly . . . !' I gasped, staring up at the monumental mountain.

But we kept moving forwards. 'Nelly!' I repeated. 'Whoa!'

I pulled on the reins, and Nelly, our giant turtle, finally came to a halt. The four of us de-turtled and thanked her for the lift.

'Watch out for the Dorcs,' she warned us. 'That mountain is swarming with them.'

'What are Dorcs?' I asked.

'Oh they used to be Orcs,' she explained. 'Stupid, primitive creatures. But something changed them into highly intelligent, socially awkward Dorcs.'

I scratched my beard thoughtfully. 'The Notion Potion perhaps . . . ?' I wondered aloud.

Nelly shrugged. Which was impressive for someone who didn't have shoulders. 'Who knows what dark magic changed them? But now they run around with their trousers pulled up to their armpits, terrifying everyone, pursuing them with annoying, trivial questions.'

'Yikes. Is there any way we can avoid

this . . . trivial pursuit*?' I asked.

'Steer clear of the mines,' she advised. 'Stick to the Cliffs of Death.'

'The Cliffs of Death – that sounds way safer! Thanks, Nelly!' I called, with a tip of my hat, and we strolled off towards the giant, treacherous mountain.

Not long after, we were up on the Cliffs of Death, getting pounded by a blizzard of doom.

'This doesn't feel very safe at all!' I shouted, over the roaring wind and snow.

We'd been trying to follow a path along the cliffs, but it had grown narrower and narrower, until we were now edging our way along it with our backs against the craggy rock.

'Yeah, this is actually quite dangerous,'

***TRIVIAL PURSUIT** – a board game where chunks of cheese are awarded for answering questions. This fun interrogation was invented by cheesemongers, the nosiest of all mongers.

agreed Crunchie, glancing down at the terrifying drop beneath us.

'You got that righty-rights! That turtle was a big galloo for sending us up here!' complained Lou.

Wilbert, whose fur was covered in ice, gave a yowl of agreement. He then gestured at his belly again, and I sighed with annoyance. 'Wilbert, does this look like a good time to you?'

Just then, there was a great gust of wind and Loopy Lou slipped off the cliff.

'Whoopsie!' he shrieked.

'Arghhh!' we all screamed.

He almost plummeted to his death, but at the last second, Lou managed to grasp the edge of the ledge we were standing on. He dangled there, clinging on by his fingers.

'Wooh!' I gasped. 'That was close.'

'Thought we'd lost you there, Lou,' chuckled Crunchie, shaking his head.

'I almost went bye-bye!' agreed Lou, looking shaken.

Wilbert licked Lou's face happily, but Lou recoiled from the Wonkey – 'Ugh! Yuck!' – and lost his grip on the ledge.

'Lou!' I cried in horror.

Down he fell, plummeting into the abyss.

'Whoopsieeeeeeeeeeeeeeeeeeeeeeeeeeeee!!!!!!!'

And as I watched him tumble through the air, I saw an enormous dragon swoop towards him, about to catch him in mid-air and devour him!

Just at that same moment, in a warm, cushy house in Boyle, Trevor had just woken up and was lying in bed feeling quite bored. He gave a yawn and then looked around for his IF.

'Lou!' he called. 'Loopy Lou! Where are you?'

And as that dragon opened its great jaws to swallow him up, Trevor imagined his trusty clown and . . .

POP!

Lou vanished from the imaginary world and . . .

POP!

. . . reappeared in Boyle. Still screaming.

'– eeeeeeeeeeeeeee!!!'

'Why are you making all that racket?' asked Trevor.

Lou opened his eyes and saw where he was.

He was too shocked to be relieved, and just stood there shaking.

'Do a dance for me,' requested Trevor.

'I almost died!' gasped Lou. 'I almost diedy-died!'

'Come on, Lou. Do a nice morning dance!'

Still trembling, and looking deathly pale, Lou obediently started to perform a dance routine. In a weak voice, he rapped as he pulled his moves: '*My name is Lou! How do you do?! I'm here for you. I'm Trevvy's crew!*'

'Wooh!' cheered a delighted Trevor, clapping for the traumatized clown.

'Thanks, Trevvy. Now, I just think I need a little lie-down,' murmured Lou, and collapsed on to the floor. 'Whoopsie,' he whispered.

Back in the imaginary world, the remaining three of us had managed to get off the treacherous Cliffs of Death and were now huddled inside a cave on the edge of Mount Figment.

'What happened to Lou?' gasped Crunchie, still catching his breath.

'Trevor must've woken up and imagined him,' I guessed.

'Lucky duck. I hope Padraic hurries up and imagines me too. I don't like this quest any more.'

The Wonkey nodded in agreement and started moaning something that sounded like '*RrrrrrMartin! Imagine us!*'

'Stop that, Wilbert!' I snapped. 'We're not going home without the Notion Potion. Now let's get moving – there's no *rest* in *quest!*'

CHAPTER FIFTEEN
THE MINES OF MISFORTUNE

Despite Wilbert's hopes, Martin was doing his very best not to imagine us, and was trying to come up with more ideas for inventions – in case we couldn't find the N.P. But his meandering mind was also wondering if it was too early to have a bath and/or a second breakfast as he paced anxiously around his bedroom.

It was a fairly small bedroom. Two beds sucked up most of the floor space, so the 'pacing-friendly' zone was quite limited. And as he went on his eighth mini-lap, his eager foot trod on something that it really should have avoided.

'Argghh! Me flippin' toe!' shrieked Sinead. 'Ya clumsy flute, that's my favourite foot finger!' she barked as she sat up angrily, pulling her throbbing big toe on to the bed.

Martin bolted his eyes shut, bracing himself for a revenge attack. But as Sinead's fist instinctively flew towards his upper body to deal a severe dead arm, it suddenly stopped, inches before impact.

'Ahhh, what's the point?' Sinead sighed, before allowing her lithe limb to flop back on the bed.

Martin slowly opened his eyes, confused by the lack of pain he was feeling.

'Ahm, I don't know why I'm telling you this, Sinead, but I think maybe you forgot to hit me?'

'I didn't forget, ya tool – I just . . . couldn't be bothered,' she replied wearily.

'Couldn't be bothered to hurt me?!' asked the puzzled boy. 'But that's basically what you live for. What's happened to Sinead? What have you done with my sister?!'

'Shut up, dumbo. I'm just . . . I dunno. I don't

feel like hitting any more. I'm listless*. I'm listless and wristless.'

'Oh,' Martin said, settling on to the edge of his bed. 'Well, I'd like to help you there, Sinead, but as you well know, being listless** is something I've never had to deal with.'

'Martin, I *lost*! I lost so badly. For you, I realize that's routine, but I've never lost a battle of the fists before. It's hit me hard. I feel like a spud in a sack who's done three rounds with Fury O'Hare.'

'I see,' Martin replied sympathetically. 'Well, I'm sure you'll trounce her next time!'

'That's the problem: I won't. I can't win. I'm going to forfeit the match.'

Martin lay back on his bed and looked up at the ceiling thoughtfully, pleased to have this distraction from trying not to imagine me. 'Well, Sinead, I'm sorry to hear you talking

***LISTLESS** - lacking energy or enthusiasm.

****LISTLESS** - being without a list.

like that. But I gotta say, I'm glad you feel you can confide in me about this. I'm familiar with setbacks, it's true. I myself have stumbled on many bumps on my merry road, so you've come to the right place for advice. I know we've had our differences through the years, but I've always seen us as birds of a feath—'

Martin turned his head to address his sorrowful sibling.

'Sinead?'

But she was gone. She'd left ages ago. In fact, by the time Martin had finished his speech, Sinead had already embarked on a quest of her own. She had decided to face her victor, Fury O'Hare.

Meanwhile, on the imaginary quest, we had abandoned the Cliffs of Death and decided to try a different route instead – through the Mines of Misfortune. These were a network of huge caves and tunnels that had been carved inside the great mountain and allowed us to climb towards the peak while avoiding the blizzard outside and the enormous dragon.

However, there was one downside: we weren't alone inside that hollow mountain. And every so often we'd hear footsteps skittering around in the shadows, or a menacing cackle coming from some dark corner.

'What was that?' whispered Crunchie nervously, glancing around.

'Crunchie!' I yelled up at him. 'Focus! Is the rope secure?'

Crunchie glanced down at Wilbert and me, as we waited on a rock far below. He held the long rope in his hands and readied himself to take the strain.

'Got it!' he called. 'Climb on up!'

I knew that the Wonkey wouldn't be able to climb the rope with his useless hoofs, so I told him to hop on my back. When he mounted me, I nearly fell flat on my face, but somehow I managed to stay on my feet, and slowly began to climb the rope.

Inch by inch, I hauled us upward, with Wilbert's front legs wrapped around my neck. I didn't dare look down at the terrifying drop beneath us. Spiky rocks protruded from the ground where armies of woodlice crawled. I know that woodlice are basically harmless, but they really freak me out. With all their little legs. And their name – they're the *lice of wood*. Tree-nits, people! That's what they are. *Tree-nits!!*

'Whatever you do, don't let go!' I hollered up at Crunchie.

'You can count on me, Sean!' he assured me.

But the person that I couldn't count on was Padraic O'Dwyer. Back home in Boyle, he'd just done his morning stretches and was now in the midst of his daily ear-pick. He rooted around with his finger for several minutes until he managed to extract an unusually large ball of wax.

'Look, Crunchie! I finally got it out!' he exclaimed. 'It's even bigger than we thought!'

He held up his finger, but there was no 'Oooh, blimey, that's a beauty!' from Crunchie, to Padraic's disappointment.

'Crunchie?' he called, as he began to imagine his IF. 'Where are you? You don't want to miss this!'

POP!

Crunchie appeared before him, holding a long rope, and . . .

'Arrrrrgghhhhh!' I shrieked, as Wilbert and I fell like stones through the great cave, plummeting towards the sharp rocks and freaky tree-nits.

But as we tumbled through the air, Wilbert stuck out his powerful back paws and managed to grab hold of a rocky outcrop. Our descent suddenly came to a halt, and now it was *me* clinging to *his* neck.

'Oh, Wilbert! Thank you! You saved us!' I gasped, and hugged him tightly. 'I knew this trip would lead to some quality Wonkey-IF time!'

He honked happily and wagged his tail.

'How can I ever repay you?' I asked.

He pointed at his udders hopefully.

'Eh. *Now?*'

But just then, we heard footsteps and evil cackles drawing closer. The Dorcs were closing in.

'Maybe later, pal. We gotta get outta here!'

We scrambled off the ledge and scampered up a set of long winding steps into the dark, emerging into another rocky chamber – but suddenly they were in front of us! I turned, and they were behind us too! They were above us, hanging from the rocks, and even underneath us – one of them was clinging to my ankle. We were surrounded by Dorcs!

CHAPTER SIXTEEN
WELL WELL WELL

The leader of the Dorcs came closer, scowling at me. He had greasy hair and there were several pens tucked neatly into his shirt pocket.

'Question one! Geography!' he squeaked in a high-pitched voice. I now remembered what Nelly had told me: after the pursuit would come the annoying trivial questions.

'What's the capital of Australia?' he demanded.

'What?'

'You heard me!'

'Eh. London?' I guessed. 'No, wait. Paris! Australian Paris! Paristralia! Kangaroos! Didgeridoo*! What was the question again?'

***DIDGERIDOO** – an Australian musical instrument. If you blow through one end, it makes a low, calming sound. But if you blow through the other end, it makes a high-pitched terrifying sound, and it's then known as a Didgeridon't.

'Incorrect!'

Wilbert gave a groan, clearly having another cheese-cramp. 'Rrrannghеrrrrrah!'

The Dorc peered at him. 'Did he just say Canberra?'

'Yes he did.'

Wilbert looked confused, and the Dorc was disappointed. 'Lucky guess.'

'Can we go now?' I asked.

'Question two. Sports and Leisure!' squeaked the Dorc. 'For which track event did Carl Lewis win a gold medal at the 1984 Olympics?'

Wilbert and I looked at each other blankly.

'RUN!' I cried.

'*Very close*, but can you be more specific?' asked the Dorc.

Wilbert pushed him aside, I leaped free from the ankle-gripping Dorc, and we bolted away. They charged after us as we sprinted through the great cave, and Wilbert gave a loud 'HEEE-HOWLLLLLLLLL!' to try to scare them off. But there were too many of them. They swarmed around us, and soon they had us cornered again, pinned against the rock.

'Imagine us, Martin! Imagine us!' I prayed.

But at that moment, Martin was furiously trying *not* to imagine us, so he didn't disrupt the quest. He was sitting in the bath, working on an idea for a new invention – a pop-up popcorn maker. Similar to a pop-up storybook, a paper saucepan would pop up from a book where you could then cook popcorn. But the idea needed more work as he'd calculated that the risk of fires was 186 per cent.

'Stay back!' I shrieked, and dug around in my adventure-backpack for a weapon. I threw the Belgian Army Fork at them, and then the tin of baked beans, but they just ducked them. Then I pulled out the tractor-shaped torch that Crunchie had given me, and shone it at them fiercely.

The Dorc leader smirked. 'You really think a tractor-shaped torch is going to scare us?'

'It's a Tractor Beam!' I retorted.

He frowned. 'A tractor beam?'

'You know – like they have on spaceships. But this is a tractor. With a beam.'

The Dorc thought about this for a moment, and then started to chuckle. Quietly at first, but then getting louder.

'Hahaha! Hahahahahaha! *A tractor beam!*' he snorted. 'That's brilliant!'

The other Dorcs started laughing too, giggling and snorting. 'Hahahahahaha! Because it's a tractor! And a torch!'

They honked and howled, falling around the cave, braying with laughter. I was a bit surprised at this – but then again, it *is* a truly excellent joke.

As they guffawed and snickered, Wilbert and I saw our chance to escape. We tiptoed away from the tittering troop and made for the stone steps. We sprinted up them as fast as we could, and then finally burst through a wooden doorway that led us back out into the open air.

We were on the peak of Mount Figment! The

blizzard had passed, and the imaginary world was spread out beneath us. The dragon circled far below, but thankfully hadn't noticed us.

'Well well well,' came a croaky, mysterious voice.

We turned to see a wrinkly old merchant standing at a cart selling Mount Figment souvenirs. He gave a crooked smile with a mouth missing several teeth.

'What seek ye, weary travellers?' He gestured to a display beside him. 'Postcards, perhaps? Two for a pound?'

'What? No, we seek the Notion Potion!'

'The Notion Potion, you say?' The old merchant chuckled to himself. 'Well well well.'

'Why do you keep saying that?'

'Because that's where you are, my friend! Welcome to the Well Well Well!'

I turned to see a small stone structure nearby and gasped with amazement. 'The imaginary well! We've found it!'

We bounded over excitedly and peered down into its dark depths, but could see nothing.

'Why is it called the Well Well Well?' I asked.

'Well, because it's a well, and it was built by two IFs called Jim Well and Mary Well. Would

you like a mug with their faces on it? It's dishwasher safe . . .' he offered.

'No thanks.'

'A nice fridge magnet then? I give a special price for you, my friend.'

'Thanks, but we're just here for the Notion Potion.'

'As you wish. You're hoping it'll make you as clever as the Orcs, I presume?'

I looked at him. 'So it *was* the Notion Potion that turned them into Dorcs! It really works then?'

The old man chuckled. 'Oh, it works all right.'

I picked up a wooden bucket that was attached to a long rope and eagerly hoisted it over the edge. Then I started to lower it down into the Well Well Well.

'Do I just help myself to as much as I want?' I asked.

The crazy old man chuckled again. 'Hahaha. *You could.* If there was anything in it.'

I paused, worried. 'What do you mean?'

'The Dorcs drank it dry many moons ago.'

I gasped. 'What?! You mean, the Well Well Well is *empty*?!'

I lost my grip on the rope, and the bucket went clattering downward. I heard it hit the ground inside the well with a dull thud. There was no splash – the old man was telling the truth. I slumped to the ground, crushed.

I couldn't believe that we'd come all this way, risking our necks on this treacherous journey, only to be denied at the very last hurdle. I don't mind telling you this, dear reader old pal – I began to sob. I sobbed like a baby. Like a big, beardy baby.

'Oh balls!' I cried. 'Balls! Balls! Baaaaaaallllllllls!!'

The old merchant looked at me sympathetically. 'You know what might make you feel better?'

'I don't want to buy any flippin' postcards!' I snapped.

'OK, how about a nice Mount Figment egg cup?'

'No!'

'A tea towel with pictures of Dorcs on it?'

'No!'

'A bottle of Notion Potion?'

'No! Wait – What?' I scrambled to my feet. 'You've got the Notion Potion?'

He grinned at me, showing his few remaining rotten teeth. 'I managed to save some before those savages guzzled it all.'

He opened his jacket and pulled out a large glass bottle with a cork in its neck. It was filled with a strange blue liquid that swirled around as magically as a lava lamp*.

'What would a weary traveller like you offer for such a drink?'

I considered all of my possessions. 'Do you want some jelly beans?' I asked.

***LAVA LAMP** – a lamp with blobs of lava bubbling inside it. It was invented when a snow globe got accidentally left inside a pizza oven.

'What I want is right in front of me,' he replied. And with a wrinkly old finger, he poked me on the chin.

'You want . . . *my face*?' I asked, alarmed. 'My beautiful face?!'

'Of course not, that would be weird! I want . . . *your beautiful beard!*'

I couldn't believe it, but the old loon was serious.

'All my life I have tried to grow a beard such as this,' he said, admiring my lush whiskers. 'Alas, nothing grows on my barren chin but pathetic peach fuzz. Oh, how I have longed for a bountiful beard such as yours!'

'But . . . my beard is like my soul! A warm, hairy, handsome soul! Can't I give you something else? How about a skipping rope?' I suggested.

'I will accept nothing but that beard!' he said firmly, tucking the bottle of Notion Potion back into his jacket. 'Take it or leave it, my friend. The choice is yours! Ahahahahahahahahahahahaha!!' he cackled, as loud as the Dorcs.

It was a strange place, this weird mountain, but at least it was filled with laughter.

CHAPTER SEVENTEEN
CAN'T LIVE WITHOUT THEM

Oblivious to my facial-hair dilemma, Martin was still sitting in the bath, and had crumpled up his plans for the pop-up popcorn maker. He then forced himself to think about pigeons so that he wouldn't imagine me. Even though I'd only been gone a few hours, this was proving to be quite the challenge, and he'd hoped that a good soak would help him forget all about his absent IF.

Martin loved baths – the suds, the calming effect of water on skin, the fun bubbles that came from submerged farts – the whole kit and caboodle*. But he had one gripe with the

***KIT AND CABOODLE** - an expression that means 'everything and more'. Coined by the wealthy Russian twins, Caboodle and Kit Shebang, who owned most things.

bathing experience: the lack of available food. He'd be happily floating or scrubbing when his tummy would rumble, or even call out 'Hey! What about me? I'm starvin' down here!'

Reluctantly he decided to abandon his cosy water hole and get himself a sandwich.

In the kitchen, he found Fidelma and his mam having a bit of a barney* about some boy.

'The big dork from the school choir?' Debra enquired.

'He's not a dork, Mam. His name is Dessie and he's lovely.'

'The holy Joe with the keyboard?' scoffed Trisha, who was making tea nearby.

'Shaddup, Trish, you're just jealous!'

'Ah, boys, boys, boys . . .' Martin nodded sagely. 'Can't live with them. That's what they say.'

***BARNEY** - a term used to describe an argument. Named after a Londoner called Barney Squabble. He was such a tricky gentleman that his name coined two terms for fightin'.

The women stared at him briefly before returning to their squabble.

During Martin's short but eventful life, he'd seen this kind of thing many times before. One of his silly sisters would fall in 'love' with some Spanish stable boy or waxy-haired drummer or (in Sinead's case) a local farmer's nephew who dressed like a scarecrow. Martin had learned it was best not to get involved, and would usually just offer wise, pointless titbits like 'Ah yeah, love is strange'. Or 'What's good for the goose . . .' Or 'Nothin' like a good chat'.

'Mam, do we have sandwich bread?' he asked.

'Or dead batteries?' enquired Trisha.

But Debra was still getting to grips with the ongoing Fidelma situation.

'Delma, this is not a good time to be gettin' involved with some fella – check the flippin' bread-bin, Martin – you've got your exams coming up, you need to stay focused right now –

most of the batteries in the press* are probably dead, Trish – and if your head drifts from your books to some piano-playin' plonker, you might never be the first female Taoiseach.'

'Well, maybe that's not what *I* want, Mam. Maybe . . .' Fidelma was getting a bit emotional now, as she gathered her books into her chest. 'Maybe that's just what *you* want!' she blubbered as she stormed out, leaving her mother at a loss for words.

Taking the difficult situation into account, Martin turned to Trisha and asked the important question: 'Why do you need dead batteries?'

'I'm making a necklace out of them.'

'But . . . they're rubbish, Trish.'

'Well, yes. And you're the one who gave me the idea for that – thanks, Martin!'

***PRESS** – in Ireland, a cupboard is called a 'press' because we hoard so much junk that the door must be *pressed* hard to stay shut.

'You're welcome?' he replied uncertainly. 'But are you not worried that people will look at you and say, "*Ah there's Trisha Moone, wearing a big head of garbage again*"?'

Trisha thought about this for a second. 'The thing is, Martin, I like my face, but I also like to have fun with it. Sometimes you can make a good thing even better.'

'Like baths!'

'What?'

'I love baths, but I wish I could make my bath even better.'

'Why do you keep saying "baths"?'

'I'd nap in a bath if it weren't so dangerous – ya know what I mean, Trish?'

But Trisha was already gone. It seemed whenever Martin was closing in on something brilliant, the ladies in his life would desert him. He turned to his mother.

'Mam, do you know how to make a waterproof sandwich?'

'No, Martin, it seems I don't know anything.'

She shook her head sadly, before deserting him.

Martin retreated to his bedroom and tried again not to imagine me. But as he lay his dopey head on his pillow for a nap, there was another rumble, and this time it wasn't his empty belly. His wardrobe shook, and he sat up.

'Sean . . . ?! Wilbert . . . ?!'

Suddenly it burst open and the Wonkey bounded into the room. He looked relieved to be back, and even more relieved that he no longer had a bulging milk-belly. But Martin was too startled to notice this as he watched me tumble out after Wilbert and fall flat on my battered back. I was exhausted. I stank of adventure. And I was completely beard-less.

CHAPTER EIGHTEEN
THE GENIUS JUICE

Martin had never seen my naked face before, so it took a moment for him to recognize me – but then his eyes lit up with delight. 'It's you, Sean! You're back!'

His gaze moved to my chin and he gave a little frown. 'Oh. So *that's* why you've always had a beard.'

'What? What do you mean?' I asked self-consciously, bringing a hand to my chin.

Martin looked at me, then back at my chin. Then at my ears, then back at my chin. Then at the floor, then back at my chin. 'Eh. Nothing,' he said to my chin, a bit flustered. He did his best not to stare at it, but I knew what was going on.

You see, for as long as I can remember,

my chin has been home to a large and rather strange-looking mole. Unlike human moles, IF moles are multicoloured, and mine was a bright lime green. There were two blue dots on its peak, and along with a few red hairs sprouting from its crown, it looked very much like a tiny face. When I was young, this face was my friend, and I named the mole 'Gerald'. But as I got older, other imaginaries would laugh at Gerald and call us names like 'Chin Face', 'Two Heads', and 'Moley-Moley-Mole-Mole'. So as soon as puberty* arrived, I decided to shield

***PUBERTY** – when children start turning into big hairy adults with smelly armpits. The term was first coined by the sister of a boy called Berty who didn't realize that it was time to start using deodorant. She held her nose and shouted, *'Peww, Berty!*

Gerald from those mocking eyes, and I hid him inside the finest forest of chin whiskers ever known. And there he stayed, in his handsome, hairy hideout, until now.

'So, eh . . . what happened on the quest? Did you find the imaginary well?' asked Martin, trying not to stare at Gerald.

'Well, Martin, I've got good news and bad news.'

'What's the good news?' he asked eagerly.

I paused. 'Sorry, I didn't think that through – I've actually only got bad news.'

Martin gaped at me (but mostly Gerald), looking like he'd been punched in the stomach. 'Oh no . . . ! You didn't find the Notion Potion?!' He reeled around, devastated. 'Now what am I going to do?! How am I going to come up with a brilliant invention without that genius juice? The Convention is just a week away, and we've got nothing but a burnt robot, a chopped-up coat, and some soggy firework boots! How's that going to beat those snarky snobs from St

Whimmion's? How's that going to get my face on the Winners Wall?'

'It wasn't my fault, Martin! Let me just tell you what happened!'

But Martin frowned, staring at my backpack. I thought he was just trying not to gawk at Gerald, but then his worried face began to brighten, and he looked at me with a broad grin.

'Oh, *you*.'

'Huh?'

He wagged his finger at me playfully. 'Sean Murphy, you big joker. You totally had me there!'

'What are ya talking about, buddy?' I asked, baffled.

'You big scamp! You cheeky monkey. You scallywag! You really got me that time! I totally believed you!'

'You believed what?'

'That you didn't get the Notion Potion!' he exclaimed, and plucked the glass bottle from my bag. This was the same bottle that the merchant had traded for my beard, but now it was filled with a dark *green* liquid.

'All this time you had it right here, ya big trickster!'

I glanced at Wilbert, and we shared a worried look. 'Eh . . .'

'Is that mole part of the joke too?' asked Martin, with a suspicious smile. 'I bet it's totally fake!'

He pinched Gerald and wiggled him about, trying to pull him off my face.

'OWW!' I yelped. 'Stop that!'

Martin's smile faded and he withdrew his hand. 'Nope, not fake. Sorry about that.'

There was an awkward pause.

'Anyhoo . . .' he continued, turning his attention back to the bottle. 'You found it! You found the Notion Potion!'

He pulled out the cork, and some strange, green steam puffed out of the bottle, wafting around his bedroom in clouds.

'Oooh, steamy!' he marvelled, his eyes dancing with excitement.

'Hang on, buddy. It's not what you think—' I began. But before I could finish, Martin was already gulping it down!

Glug, glug, glug – the entire bottle disappeared down his gullet in seconds!

'Martin, wait! You *really* don't want to drink that – let me explain!'

But Martin just swallowed and cried out, 'Wooooh! That. Is. *Tangy**!'

He gasped, panting. 'It's like there's a fizzy rollercoaster in my mouth. Made of butter and grapefruits and mackerel and sweaty cheese.'

'Wow, that's a really . . . complex flavour.'

Martin swished it around his mouth. 'It's also quite warm.'

Wilbert and I looked at each other uneasily.

Martin stood there for a moment, waiting.

'I think something's happening!' he exclaimed suddenly. 'It must be starting to work!'

'Are you sure?' I asked doubtfully.

He belched, jiggled his head, jumped in the air, and then yelped, 'I've got it!'

'Got what?!'

He cartwheeled over to his desk, grabbed a

***TANGY** – sharp and bitter. Like a dangerously pointy lemon.

crayon from the floor, and suddenly began to scrawl on the wall!

In a wild frenzy, he scribbled down formulas, mathematical equations and strange squiggles and doodles. His hand was a blur as he feverishly covered the old wallpaper with complicated diagrams and blueprints for an invention.

I tried to interrupt a few times to explain what had happened on the quest, but Martin was lost in his thoughts, muttering to himself as he worked.

He didn't stop until every inch of wallpaper was covered with his ideas. And after using up three crayons, two markers, and a pencil, he finally whispered, 'It is done.'

Completely drained, he face-planted on to his bed and fell fast asleep.

Res[f(z);-i]
Mc=

CHAPTER NINETEEN
TUB GRUB

Martin slept for the rest of that afternoon. Normally he avoided napping, as it left him vulnerable to attacks from Sinead, and he'd often woken up to find himself graffitied with make-up – but thankfully his sister was nowhere near his sleeping face. Her quest, or more accurately, the bus, had taken her to sunny South Roscommon, where she found herself peeking through the window of Let's Talk Some Scents.

Fury O'Hare was in the midst of sculpting a bouquet of seasonal Roscommon flowers. Dandelions, crabgrass and pigweed were strewn on the dainty florist's floor. Sinead hid outside, nervously watching her preen and prune.

All of a sudden, the mighty warrior halted

her work, smelt the air and whispered, 'I find conversation works best when people are in the same room, young Moone.'

Impressed but intimidated, Sinead slipped gingerly into the shop (which was difficult because the door had a bell, which chimed loudly on entry).

'Sorry to disturb you, Mrs O'Hare, but I've come to concede,' she mumbled.

'Concede?'

Sinead nodded solemnly. 'Sometimes you gotta know when you're beat. You deserve the sack-punching crown. There's no need for us to battle again.'

Fury looked surprised, but nodded sagely.

'Yes. It is true, young Moone, that if we were to battle again right now, you would be bested.'

'I know, that's why I'm forfeiting.'

'Perhaps . . .' O'Hare mused, as she edged towards Sinead. 'Perhaps it would be better if we used eggs instead of potatoes?'

'Eggs?'

'Yes, because it seems you are . . . a chicken, no?'

'I'm not a ch— . . . I get it, OK? You're better than me. Just shake my hand and accept my forfeit so I can get on with my life.'

The florist looked at Sinead's outstretched hand and the beaten expression on her face. She softened and wilted, like a tulip in June.

'You have skill, young Moone. But you are wild, like a flower in a desert. You need to become like a single white rose in a vase. Sharp, but striking.'

'But I've trained so hard already – I don't think—'

'Silence! The mistake every novice makes is thinking that practice makes perfect. But only *perfect* practice makes perfect. You need teaching.'

'You?'

'No – fat Freddy in the flippin' newsagent's next door! Yes, me! I shall teach you. You will be my apprentice. And you will soon learn that to beat the potato, you must *become* the potato!'

Something odd was happening on Sinead's face. Her mouth was contorting into a strange, rarely seen shape. It was a smile.

*

At that same moment, Martin's mouth was contorting into a much uglier shape. 'Aaarrggh, me head feels like a bag of snakes,' he grumbled, as groggy as a seasick toad.

'Well, you haven't moved for hours!' I told him.

His eyes slowly squinted open to find the Wonkey and me peering down at him. All that thinking seemed to have worn him out, like his head jelly had run a mind-marathon – and he closed his eyes again.

'C'mon, Martin! Time to wake up. We need to do something about these drawings.'

'What drawings?'

As I pointed to the scribble-covered walls, the bedroom door burst open, revealing a bewildered Mammy Moone.

'Oh balls,' we whispered in unison.

'Martin, what the flip did you do to your room?'

Martin was a terrible liar at the best of times, and with his mind still in recovery mode, his deception skills were even weaker than usual.

'It's . . . Modern Art?'

'Well, get your arse out of bed and your art off those walls,' Debra snapped, before leaving in a huff to do whatever nonsense it is that mothers do.

'What *is* all this stuff?' asked Martin, as he stumbled to his feet and examined the wall scrawls.

'It's your "big idea that'll change the world".'

'It is . . . ?' he asked, staring at the strange scribbles. 'Wait – Of course! I drank the Notion Potion you brought back from the quest, turned into a genius, and came up with an incredible invention!'

'Ehh. Well, you drank *something*,' I began hesitantly, 'and went kinda mad. That's what I've been trying to tell you, buddy. To be honest, I think you might have been allergic to it. I mean, you *are* allergic to a lot of stuff. Strawberries. Silk. Bees . . .'

But Martin wasn't listening; he was staring at

the weird writing. 'Hmmm. I better show this to the team!' he said, and started ripping down the sheets of wallpaper.

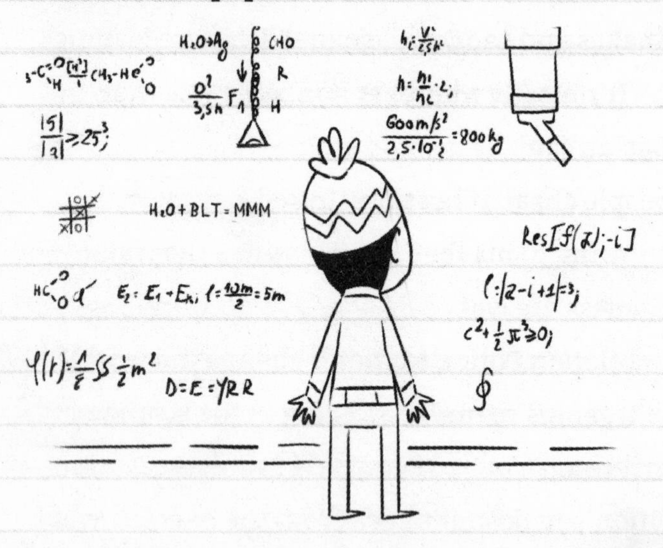

Martin brought his plans to the rest of Team Trepdem, confident that their collective brain-power would sort through the strange squiggles and discover the genius within.

'I think that bit is . . . a rabbit's face, but it's wearing . . . a purple party hat?'

Padraic was pointing at a particularly confusing segment of the plans. The others were squinting and tilting their heads, trying to make sense of the wall scrawls that were laid out on the ground.

'This bit looks like an unfinished game of Snakes and Ladders,' observed Trevor.

'It's mostly numbers and squiggles, Martin,' Declan said. 'Is it some kind of invention to help people cheat at horse racing?'

'Ahm . . . maybe?' replied Martin, genuinely clueless. He was feeling rather annoyed that the Notion Potion hadn't made him enough of a genius to understand his own ingenious invention.

'This makes *zero* sense,' stated Trevor. 'And yet, there are so many zeroes written here.'

Team Trepdem was stumped. Martin sighed with frustration, and kicked the useless sheets of wallpaper, disappointed that they were still no closer to success. But as the sheets fell over one another, he suddenly spotted a pattern.

'Wait a second . . .'

He began to line up the bits of wallpaper in

a different order, like he was piecing together a puzzle. Somehow, he seemed to be reading it and making sense of it.

'Oh you clever little sausage, haha . . . Oh that's good, yes!' He chuckled to himself, as the others watched in bewilderment. 'I gotta tell ya, folks, I'm impressed.'

'By what?' asked the boys.

'By *whom* should be the question. And the answer is . . . by myself! I *knew* I hadn't imagined it! I *am* a genius! And my world-changing invention is all right here in front of us!'

'What is it?' Trevor begged, instantly excited.

'Hmmm. Where to start . . .' Martin mused, smiling smugly at his friends. 'You sure you'll be able to keep up?'

'Start talkin' or start hurtin', Moone,' growled a looming Declan.

Martin stroked his chin, like he imagined all great inventors did. 'OK. Let me try to explain my wondrous new creation in layman's terms*.'

'Spit it out, Moone,' Declan threatened, 'before I spit *you* out.'

'Your impatience is justified, Mr Mannion. If I were you, I too would be shaking with excitement.'

'I'll shake *you* with excitement,' Declan growled.

'Okey-doke. Here we go. Who among us enjoys baths?'

The team tentatively raised their hands.

'And when you're in the bath, but suddenly get peckish – what do you do?'

The others grumbled, agreeing that this was a nuisance.

'Just this morning I was having a nice soak in the suds,' continued Martin, 'when I started

***LAYMAN'S TERMS** – when an expert has to explain something complicated to a non-expert, they often use 'layman's terms'. It's the process of making simple a complicated idea to a man who is laying down, or even half asleep.

craving a snack. So like a soapy sap, I had to get *out* of the bath to make myself a sandwich!'

'Oh, tell me about it! It's such a pain,' agreed Padraic. 'What I do now is cook my dinner before I get in, and then serve myself inside the bath. But it's still far from problem-free. The other day, my cottage pie fell into the water and I was fishing around for it for ages, and it got so soggy and soapy that I nearly couldn't eat it – a total nightmare!'

'Well, the nightmare ends here!' declared Martin.

'The nightmare of you talking about baths?' asked Declan.

'The contents of these wallpaper drawings
will change the way we look at bathing.
And change the way we look at food.
Because my invention kills two birds with
one stone.'

'That's good maths,' noted Padraic.

'Instead of bringing a snack into the bath, the snack *is* the bath. You bathe *in* your snack!

Instead of a *soapy* bath, you can take a *soupy* bath!'

'Like . . . edible bath salts?' Trevor asked.

'It's so much more than that, Trev.'

'Bath salts . . . and pepper?'

'Well, sure, if that's the only flavour you enjoy. But my invention allows the bather to create a Readybix bath! Or a cheesecake, or lasagne bath! You can wash yourself in tea! Or honey! Or yogurt! The possibilities are endless!'

'Like . . . having soda streams instead of taps?' Padraic asked.

'Now you're getting it, P,' said Martin. 'And have I mentioned that this bath will also be portable?'

'What?' the now riveted group gasped.

'This will be a *mobile* bath, because, quite frankly, people will want it wherever they go! Be it beach parties, sporting events, religious festivals . . .'

'It'll be like the St Whimmion's fancy bus bath!' cried Padraic.

'Yes!' agreed Trevor. 'But way better, cos of . . . the bath food!'

'Eating in the bath *would* be kinda handy, to be fair,' muttered Declan, with a shrug. But the others were blown away.

'Everyone will be green with envy when they see me wallowing in my raspberry ripple ice-cream bath!' shrieked Trevor.

'I love it, Martin!' Padraic cheered, as he patted his buddy on the back. 'It's like a mobile . . . flavour bath!'

'That's right. I call it the Tub Grub 2000!'

CHAPTER TWENTY
OPERATION BATH BUILD

I still hadn't had a chance to explain to Martin what had happened on the quest, but when I saw how excited he was about his new idea, I began to wonder if telling him the truth was really the right thing to do. Why burst his bubble? Why cause trouble? Or do other stuff that rhymes with 'ubble'? The reason that we went looking for the Notion Potion in the first place, was to bring him inspiration, and even if we hadn't *quite* succeeded, the boy was most definitely inspired! And deluded too, I suppose – since he now thought he was some kind of mad genius. But hey, at least now they had an idea – of sorts.

And over the next few days, Team Trepdem got stuck into the task of turning that weird bath idea into the most exciting invention to ever hit the world of damp-dining.

Martin doled out tasks to them all, and the vital job of finding an old bath was given to Declan Mannion. Martin suggested checking the town junkyard, but instead Declan simply took a hammer and a wrench, and turned his own family's bathroom into a bathlessroom – to the dismay of his poor, suds-loving dad.

Another dejected dad was Liam Moone, as the team had completely taken over his workshop. Liam had foolishly agreed to play a game of poker with Declan and had lost his coat, his treasured handball*, and all rights to his workshop. So while Declan paraded around in Liam's favourite jacket, bouncing his handball, the team got to work on transforming the Mannion tub.

Since the invention was Martin's idea, it was agreed that he should be in charge, and he took to leadership like a duck to ducktatorship, quacking orders at everyone.

'No, that doesn't go there; it goes over *there*!' he yelled at Padraic.

'Those screws need to be flat!' he shouted at

*__HANDBALL__ – a ball used in the sport of handball**.

**__HANDBALL__ – very similar to football. But instead of feet, soft goal-nets and the sound of cheering fans, it involves hands, concrete walls and the cheers of absolutely nobody.

Trevor. 'I want this bath to be aerodynamic*!'

'Declan, why are you reading the *Racing News*? It's not your break-time yet!'

'I think you'll find that it *is* my break-time, Moone,' replied Declan, with a menacing look. 'It's *always* my break-time.'

'My mistake. Carry on, Declan.'

Despite Declan's never-ending breaks and constant reminders that this project had better pay him some gold soon, the Tub Grub 2000 gradually began to take shape. It was exciting to watch, and Martin's hopes were growing for both the Invention Convention and the Winners Wall.

'This is all thanks to you, Sean,' he whispered to me one day. 'I never could have come up with this if I hadn't drunk the N.P.!'

***AERODYNAMIC** – when air flows around an object smoothly so it can move faster. This was found to be important after the surprising slowness of the world's first racing car, which was a perfect cube.

At least, that's what he *thought* he'd drunk. But the Wonkey and I knew better.

'Sean, I beseech you!' whispered Wilbert. 'You can't let this go on any longer. The boy deserves to know the truth.'

I still hadn't got used to the fact that Wilbert could talk now – another unexpected result of our failed quest.

'Quiet, you!' I hissed. 'I tried to tell him before, but it's too late now. If Martin finds out the truth at this stage, he'll go bananas. And besides, he doesn't seem to care what happened on the quest or that we risked our necks for him – all he cares about is his invention. He hasn't even noticed that you've been milked! So let's just keep our traps shut. You especially. And act more Wonkeyish! Chase your bum or something!'

Wilbert gave a weary sigh, and then proceeded to jog around in circles, pretending to pursue his buttocks.

*

Being in charge was a new experience for Martin, and every day he grew bossier and more demanding, relishing his position of power. He also grew smellier, as he'd stopped washing himself and let his hair become as wild as Albert Einstein*'s mad mop, keen to look the part of the mad inventor. He stopped trimming his fingernails too, which grew long like those of Howard Hughes**, and looked like claws as he clutched his wallpaper plans, shouting, 'Build, lads! Build my bath! Bring her to life!' like a young Dr Frankenstein***.

'I have an announcement to make, team! I don't want you to call me "Martin Moone" any more!' he declared one day. 'It's about time that I had a catchy nickname like "the Mad Mechanic". So from now on, you can call me . . . "the Batty Bathman"!'

***ALBERT EINSTEIN, **HOWARD HUGHES, ***DR FRANKENSTEIN** – three mad scientists. A history maker, an aeroplane maker, and a (fictional) monster maker. One of them was also an excellent fairy-cake maker, but I can't remember which one.

'I love it, Martin!' cried Padraic, as he worked a blowtorch on the bath. 'And I'll be "the Whimsical Welder"!'

'No, *you* don't have a nickname; you're just the welder,' snapped Martin.

'Okey-doke!' replied Padraic brightly. '"No Nickname Padraic", that's what you can call me!'

'Wait a second – what are you doing?'

Martin was staring at the bath and realized that Padraic had welded three large Taste Tanks to the wrong end of it.

'No no no! That's all backwards! You can't just lash on the Taste Tanks willy-nilly – there's an art to this, Padraic! We're not throwing together some kind of bargain-basement bath canteen! This is the Tub Grub 2000! This is the next must-have invention of the world! But not if it looks like some kind of sloppy, souped-up bath with a few wheels stuck to it!'

'But Martin—'

'Batty Bathman!'

'But Batty Bathman,' continued Padraic, 'there's too many large Taste Tanks on one side. It'll be off balance and could topple over when it's on the move. And besides, does it really matter if they're here or there?'

'*Does it matter?!*' asked Martin incredulously, scratching his head where flies were buzzing in his matted mop. 'Does it matter if the bicycle has nine saddles and one wheel? Or if the airplane has fifty-two wings shaped like trumpets? Or if the kettle is built out of gorgonzola cheese?' he asked, glaring at Padraic with a demented look in his eyes. 'Yes it DOES matter!'

Padraic looked at his friend, a bit concerned. 'Are you OK, Martin? I mean, Batty Bathman. Maybe you should get some rest.'

'And a wash,' muttered Trevor.

'And maybe you two should follow my instructions and stop making a hames of* my genius invention!' retorted Martin.

'Well, they're welded now,' pointed out Trevor. 'Can't we just leave them there?'

In a sudden (and quite impressive!) move, Martin karate-kicked the newly welded Taste Tanks, sending them clattering off the bath.

***MAKING A HAMES OF** - making a mess of. Named after Henry Hames, who was the clumsiest man in Ireland and spent most of his life trying to get his head out of a bucket.

However, he hadn't realized that one of the tanks was filled with fizzy orange, and it now sprayed all over him like the blowhole of a fizz-filled whale.

'That was *your* fault! You're fired!' yelled a drenched and sticky Martin. 'You're both fired!'

'You can't fire us!' snapped Trevor. 'We're the only ones doing any work here!'

'You think I need you? *I'm* the inventor! *I'm* the Batty Bathman!'

Padraic threw down his welder in annoyance. 'You know what? Fine! I've had it up to the wazoo with all your orders. You're on your own, Bathman. I quit!'

'Me too!' agreed Trevor.

'Me too!' blurted Declan, suddenly waking up from his fourth nap of the day. 'With pepperoni!'

'You're quitting as well?' asked Martin.

'Eh. Sorry, I thought we were ordering pizzas. But yeah, sure, I quit,' said Declan with a shrug. He rolled off the couch and followed Padraic and Trevor outside. 'But you still owe me that gold, Moone!' he called. 'And that pizza!'

Declan slammed the door shut and the trio of Tre, P and De stormed off leaving M all alone with a head filling with regrets and a face fizzing with Fanta.

CHAPTER TWENTY-ONE
THE TRUTH BOMB

It was the day after the Trepdem fallout, and Martin was absolutely miserable. He was lying on his bedroom floor, dejected, and as I stood over him, an old Realsie phrase came to mind: 'Never kick a man when he's down.' Obviously, I wasn't about to kick him. For one thing, that's forbidden in the 'IF Regulations for Reasonable Regard of Realsies'.

IF Regulations for Reasonable Regard of Realsies

Rule 17. Never kick your Realsie, especially when they're down.

Rule 18. Never pretend that you're really a ghost.

Rule 19. Never tell your Realsie to set stuff on fire.

Rule 20. Never show them your weird gills.

But I feared that what I was about to do to Martin would *feel* like a kick. A kick of words to his puny, defenceless ears. You see, I'd decided to tell him the truth. The Wonkey had talked me into it, and I suspected that this truth bomb would not explode into confetti and gumdrops and fill his heart with joy. It would be more like a stink bomb of filthy facts and rotten revelations, and I certainly didn't fancy dropping it on him when he was already down.

But then again, maybe more bad news might actually make him feel better. Two negatives make a positive, right? Or do two negatives start a family and make lots of baby negatives? Who knows . . . ? But I was about to find out.

'Martin, there's something I've got to tell you.'

He looked up. 'Did the guys come back?' he asked hopefully.

'Eh . . . No.'

'Did all the other teams get disqualified from the Invention Convention except for us?'

'That seems unlikely.'

'Did you and the other imaginaries sneak into the workshop and secretly finish building the Tub Grub 2000?'

'Em. Nope, we can't really do that, since we're . . . imaginary.'

'But you've got *good* news, right, Sean? Surely you wouldn't tell me any *bad* news right now?'

I gulped, and carried on. 'Well, Martin, I did try to tell you earlier, but . . . the truth is . . .'

My throat went dry, and I glanced at the Wonkey. He gave a supportive look and tried to do an encouraging thumbs-up, which was a bit tricky with a hoof. It just looked like he was pointing at the ceiling, which confused me a bit.

'The truth is what?' asked Martin.

'The truth is . . . I, eh . . . I actually forget what I was going to say now! Isn't that weird? Hahaha!' I laughed loudly at a baffled Martin.

Wilbert glared at me. 'Oh, spit it out, Sean! You can't keep deceiving the boy!'

Martin stared at Wilbert in amazement. 'You can talk now?'

'Oh, he's a great talker! And an even better truth-teller!' I added, edging away. 'So I'm now going to hand this over to Wilbert to continue. And I'll just be under here . . .' I said, diving under the bed, 'organizing these dust balls!'

Wilbert sighed and turned back to Martin. 'Very well. I shall tell you the truth myself.'

The Wonkey sat down on a chair and pulled out a pipe from somewhere in his matted fur. He puffed on it a few times, and then began his story.

He told Martin about everything that had happened on the quest – about Nelly, the Dorcs, the old merchant at the Well Well Well, and how I had traded my beard for a bottle of Notion Potion.

''Twas late in the day when we descended from the peak of Mount Figment,' recounted Wilbert. 'Sean and I were both feeling upbeat and triumphant. We had successfully secured the genius juice, although Sean had paid a dear price with the loss of his beard and the exposure of his hideous mole.'

'Don't call Gerald that!' I snapped from under the bed.

Wilbert ignored me and carried on.

'At the Figment foothills, we found the magical turtle Nelly waiting for us, and climbed aboard her magnificent shell. We rode south for many hours through the great Desert of Doziness. The night grew hot and humid, and I found myself overcome with a powerful thirst.'

Martin gaped up at him, listening to every word.

'I'm not proud of what I did, Martin, and I dare say that I didn't give two hoots about how much you needed that drink. I simply seized the nearest beverage within reach – which happened to be your Notion Potion – and brought the bottle to my parched lips.'

'You drank it?!' gasped Martin.

Wilbert gave a regretful nod. 'Every drop.'

'How *could* you, Wilbert?!' Martin wailed in despair.

'Yeah, Wilbert, how *could* you?' I sniped accusingly from under the bed.

Martin turned to me angrily. 'And where were *you* when this happened?'

'Don't blame *me*! I was asleep! I always fall asleep on turtles. Those shells are surprisingly comfy.'

Martin shook his head in frustration and turned back to Wilbert who continued his tale.

'What happened next is a bit of a blur. My

toes started to spasm. My ears popped. I did a small barf in my mouth. And then suddenly my head was filled with all the wisdom of the world. And like your story of the Salmon of Knowledge, it was the wrong person who'd been given this gift. I was like the young servant boy, Fionn mac Cumhaill, who poked the fish and accidentally gained all of its powers.'

Martin stood up and paced around, trying to make sense of all this. 'But – I don't understand. You *brought back* the Notion Potion. The bottle was full! Did you go back up the mountain?'

The Wonkey shook his head. 'When Sean awoke and realized what had happened, he was furious. We talked about going back, but without a spare beard, we knew we'd get nothing from the old merchant.'

'From now on, I'm never going *anywhere* without a spare beard!' I vowed.

'We carried on towards home in defeat,' continued Wilbert. 'I still needed to be milked, but Sean was too angry to do it for me. And so, using my newfound intelligence and the remaining supplies in the adventure-backpack, I built a contraption to milk myself, and refilled the empty potion bottle.'

Martin's jaw dropped. 'Oh, good gravy. So that's what I drank?! *Wonkey milk?!'*

At this point, I was trying to crawl quietly out of the bedroom, but Martin grabbed me by the ankles and yanked me back. 'Sean Murphy! Why didn't you tell me the truth?'

'I tried,' I whimpered. 'But before I could get a word out, you were already chugging down the bottle. And the weird thing, Martin, was that it kinda worked! I mean, it *didn't* work, since it was just Wonkey milk – and *imaginary* Wonkey milk, at that – but you *thought* it was Notion Potion, and so you *thought* you'd become a genius! And that was all you needed, Martin. That gave you the confidence to write up your ideas for the Tub Grub 2000 – ideas that were already in the back of your mind anyway. So in a weird way, the quest succeeded! It helped you unleash your idea. And that's all that really matters – right?'

Martin glared at me and then sank down on his bed, looking defeated. 'All this time I thought I was a genius,' he muttered. 'But I was just an idiot.'

'I'm sorry I kept the truth from you, buddy,' I told him. But he didn't even look at me. He just stared at the ground.

'Out, Sean,' he muttered.

'Out . . . ? Of your room?'

'Out of my imagination.'

'But, Martin—'

POP.

I vanished from sight.

'Well, that's that,' said Wilbert, looking refreshed. 'At least now you know the truth, and I can drop the charade of acting like a dopey animal trying to lick my own armpits. Now I can just smoke my pipe, read philosophy and ponder the meaning of life. I might start work

on a new opera too. A playful, little burletta*
about our jaunt to Mount Figment—'

POP.

Martin was alone now.

He picked up the empty bottle of Notion Potion and flung it across the room. It hit the wall and smashed into a million imaginary pieces.

***BURLETTA** - a mix of comedy and classical music where stand-up comedians belt out powerful solos, and violinists tell rude jokes about three pianists who walk into a bar.

CHAPTER TWENTY-TWO

ROUND TWO

Feeling betrayed by his trusty BIF (me) and abandoned by his friends (TrePDe), Martin was quite down in the dumps. And since his sister Trisha had basically become a walking rubbish bin, it was starting to feel like he was actually *living* in a dump. Her junk jewellery was stinking up the Moone home, so Liam strongly encouraged her to try selling her creations to the neighbours.

Trisha liked the sound of starting her own business and was soon going door-to-door with her trash trinkets. This was met with some befuddlement, but she also made several sales. She was lucky enough to catch Debra's friend Linda in a very generous mood as she sipped her fourth glass of wine. She bought a necklace made from old crisp packets, some tuna-can earrings, and even one of Trisha's ankle-bracelets made from a plastic six-pack ring.

Her biggest seller was definitely her 'Power Tie'. Businessmen love a power tie. It's basically a tie that's a strong, bold colour (usually red) and seems to yell 'I'm the boss!' But Trisha's Power Ties had a unique twist. They were made out of batteries – which *doubled* their power! They were *Power-Power Ties*. And soon, every business person in Boyle wanted one.

To Liam's bewilderment, his friends Gerry Bonner, Jim Mannion and weird Frank each ordered one. Bridget Cross, the butcher queen, and Martin's school principal, Mr Maloney, both ordered two. Francie Feeley, the stinky fish king, wanted three, and the town mayor ordered six!

Trisha was selling them as fast as she could make them, and it wasn't long before Martin found himself fruitlessly jabbing

"MOONE STYLE"

buttons on the TV remote.

'Mam, Trisha nicked the batteries again! How am I supposed to change the channel?'

'Just get up and change it, ya lazy leech,' snorted Trisha, who was taping together her third Power-Power Tie of the evening.

'Get up and change it? Like I'm living in the

flippin' Bronze Age*?! I refuse to do it!'

Trisha shrugged. 'Fine. Then just sit there and watch *Winning Streak.*'

'Fine!' snapped Martin, as the game-show began. He yelled at his parents who were sitting at the table with Fidelma. 'You see what your daughter has done to me? I'm watching *Winning Streak* over here! This is my life now! I've officially hit rock bottom!'

But his parents ignored his complaints, deep in conversation with their first-born.

'I'm sorry if you feel that we've been pushing you too hard, love,' Debra was saying, 'but you're so talented, and so clever. You've always been . . . *the special one.*'

Trisha turned to them, taken aback. '*Mam!*'

'Oh. Sorry. I meant – you're *all* special!'

***BRONZE AGE** – definitely one of the top three Ages. Just not *quite* as good as the Gold Age or Silver Age. (Although there's rumours that Gold and Silver took Age-enhancing substances.)

clarified Debra. She then leaned closer to Fidelma and whispered, 'But not as special as you.'

'We can still hear you!' snapped Martin.

'Then turn up the TV!' suggested his dad.

'I would if I could! But Trisha's Power Ties have made me powerless!'

Liam rolled his eyes and turned back to Fidelma. 'Look, Delma, you've been working so hard, and we just don't want you to have any . . . *distractions.* I mean, you're the sort of person who could do anything.'

'Even date Dessie Dolan?'

'Anything except that.'

'But I'm in love with him!' wailed Fidelma.

'Ahh – *love,*' Martin said sagely. 'It's not a hole, but we all fall into it. What a mystery!'

'Martin!' snapped his mother.

'Love is strange all right,' admitted Liam.

'Dessie won't distract me,' insisted Fidelma. 'And even if we're dating, that doesn't mean I'm going to fail my exams.'

'We know that,' Debra assured her. 'But

these exams are just a first step, and we don't want any dorky boys getting in the way of your career.'

'Mam, I know you want me to be the first female Taoiseach and all that, and maybe some day I'll do that. But just . . . not right now. OK?'

Debra looked disappointed, but gave a sigh of acceptance.

'I'm still the special one though – right?' asked Fidelma with a smile.

'Oh, definitely,' said Liam, nodding.

'Of course,' agreed Debra, then glanced at the other young Moones who did not look impressed. 'Of course you're all equals!' she added hastily.

Meanwhile, the third Moone sister had been training hard under the watchful eyes of Fury O'Hare. She had meditated, pruned Bonsai trees*, waxed on and waxed off Fury's flower

***BONSAI TREES** – tiny trees that are often grown by short people to help them feel larger and more confident.

van, learned how to jig, and balanced sacks of potatoes on her head, until finally she whispered, 'I *am* the potato.'

'Then you are ready, young Moone, and not a moment too *soon*,' rhymed her master, 'for *tonight* . . . we *fight*. *Right* at mid*night*.'

Sinead frowned. 'I thought it started at eight?'

'Sorry yes – eight. It's a *date!*' cried Mrs O'Hare, and disappeared mysteriously behind some ferns.

Who knows if Sinead had truly 'become' a potato or not, since she had no idea what that even meant, but she'd definitely improved at smashing them. And that night, as she took to the stage of the Roscommon Town Hall for Round Two, she was feeling pretty confident.

Her family were all there again in their ringside seats, ready to cheer her on. And even though Liam was feeling a bit resentful for being fired as coach, he still wore a T-shirt that said 'Mash it, Moone!'

'Thanks for coming out again, folks, and supporting the second round of the Sack-Punching Championships!' cried the priest in the red sparkly jacket to the packed crowd. 'Last time you helped raise enough funds to put a roof on the church toilet. And tonight – we've raised enough money for three of the walls!'

A big cheer went up from the crowd, and the priest continued. 'To be honest, we probably should've *started* with the walls, because that new roof fell down pretty quickly. So let's keep those donations coming in so we can get a fourth wall, another new roof, and fix the toilet that the last new roof broke!'

There were mutters from the crowd of 'Who cares?', 'Get off the stage', and 'I love that jacket'.

'All right, folks, I can sense your restlessness, so without further ado, LET'S SACK-PUNCH!!!!'

The bell rang and the battle began.

From the first moments, it was clear that Sinead was in much better shape. She was fitter and more focused, working her way around the sack methodically, smashing potato after potato. Soon, she was far in the lead – but that wasn't too hard since her opponent was doing absolutely nothing!

Fury just stood there with her eyes closed. The crowd howled and hollered, urging her to fight, but the old florist was deep in concentration. Sinead was halfway through her sack before Mrs O'Hare's arms began to move.

She raised them up slowly, and then lifted one of her legs, forming a kind of 'crane' pose as she concentrated.

Then suddenly Fury channelled every ounce of her strength into one extraordinary punch.

'HIYEEAGGHHHHHHHHHH!!!!' she screamed, as she struck the sack of potatoes. She belted that bag with such force that she obliterated every potato inside it. The whole hall trembled, and everyone stared in stunned silence.

Even Sinead was gobsmacked.

Then the bell rang, the crowd cheered, and Fury was crowned the Sack-Punching Champion of Roscommon.

'Why did you do that?' asked Sinead bitterly as they walked off the stage. 'If you knew you could win, why didn't you just let me forfeit?'

Fury smirked at her. 'Because, young Moone, I wanted to beat you properly. It's no fun winning unless someone else gets to *really lose*.'

Sinead bristled at this. 'You know what? I lied. I'm not the potato. *You're* the potato.'

'I know I'm the potato – that's how I *beat* the potato.'

'What? No, you're the potato because you're nothing but an aul lump! And you're a cowardly yellow inside. And you've got a black heart!'

Fury frowned. 'A potato doesn't have a black heart.'

'Sometimes it has black bits inside it!' retorted Sinead. 'And that's your heart! As black as a potato's black bits!'

'Oh come on, Moone, don't be a sore loser. You can try again next year. I've never battled anyone as strong as you. You made it so much more enjoyable.' Fury smiled at her sweetly. 'Let's do this again. I'd really like that.'

'Well, in that case . . . I'm retiring!' announced Sinead defiantly. 'Forever!' And with that, she walked away.

Fury's smile vanished.

'You're a sack-puncher, Sinead! What else are you going to do with your life?'

'I'll think of something.'

'Don't you walk out on me. I'm Fury O'Hare! Get back here!'

But Sinead just grinned to herself and strolled off with her head held high – not quite a winner, not quite a loser, and not quite a potato.

CHAPTER TWENTY-THREE
THE FINISHER

Martin was relieved that two of his sisters had lost some of their swagger and weren't poking fun at his puny achievements any more, but he was also aware that his own goals remained as un-scored as ever. And as he stood in the workshop, looking down at their half-finished invention, he was full of regrets.

'This could've been so great,' he murmured, 'if I hadn't messed it all up.'

He picked up a dented Taste Tank from the floor where his wallpaper plans lay abandoned, and shook his head sadly.

'Another few days and we could've finished it,' he sighed.

'Well . . . you still *can* finish it, buddy.'

He turned to see me standing behind him.

'Sean! What are you doing here?'

I shrugged. 'You imagined me.'

He smiled, glad to see me again. 'You've got your beard back,' he noted, admiring my new bristles that were now keeping Gerald nice and warm.

'Yep, that's all I've been doing ever since you kicked me out of your imagination,' I grumbled. 'Just sitting around, growing my beard.'

Martin's smile faded and he looked rather guilty. 'I'm sorry, Sean. I never should've blamed you for the Wonkey milk mix-up. It wasn't your fault that I drank it. You were just trying to help me. You went to the ends of your world and risked everything just to find some Notion Potion to help me invent an invention and get my face on the Winners Wall. You're a good friend, Sean. A good egg. A good IF.'

My grumpiness evaporated and I grinned back at him. There was no doubt that my Realsie was an idiot, but at least he knew when he was wrong.

'Ya know, Martin, the funny thing is . . . you

didn't even *need* any Notion Potion. You came up with that Tub Grub invention all on your own. All you needed was your own silly noggin,' I told him, tapping him on the forehead.

'*And* the best damn science team in the west of Ireland,' he added.

'Well yes, that too.'

Martin gazed down sadly at their abandoned tools. 'Padraic is the only one who knew how to handle that blowtorch properly . . .'

'Yeah, after losing most of his eyebrows, he finally got the hang of it all right.'

'. . . And nobody could keep track of the measurements like Trevor,' continued Martin, picking up a tape-measure. 'And of course, Declan is the only one who could find the perfect-sized Taste Tanks that offer plenty of storage while also avoiding a sense of the bath being cluttered.'

He hung his head sadly. 'You know, Sean, I don't think I ever realized how good they were – until I'd lost them.'

I nodded. 'Well, buddy, sometimes working in a team can be tricky. Maybe you're more of a lone wolf.'

He thought about this for a moment. 'No – if there's one thing I know, Sean, it's that two heads are better than one – even when one is imaginary,' he added with a grin. 'And with a team of heads, I think we can do almost anything.'

I smiled. 'Even complete a revolutionary snack'n'suds system, transport it to Dublin by tomorrow at noon, and win the biggest junior science competition in the country?'

'Why not?' replied Martin, growing in confidence.

'Why not indeed?' I agreed.

'It's not time to throw in the towel. It's time to throw *out* the towel!'

He picked up a greasy towel and chucked it out the door into the garden. 'Out with ya, towel!' he shouted. 'Martin Moone isn't beaten yet. I'm not a quitter! I'm a doer! I'm a get-stuff-doner. I'm a finisher!'

His mother peered out the kitchen window. 'Who ya talking to, love?'

'Oh, just the towel, Mam!' he called, and turned back to me. 'It's time to get back to work. I need to reform Team Trepdem. But they're all mad at me, Sean. So how can I get them all back together to apologize?'

I scratched my fresh bristles. 'Oh, I'm sure I can think of something . . .'

Martin smiled, pleased to have his wingman back at his side.

'I missed you, beardo.'

'Right back at ya, shorty,' I replied, and we high-fived happily.

*

An hour later, Padraic, Trevor and Declan Mannion rushed into Martin's back garden from different directions.

'Where's my banoffi pie*?' gasped Padraic.

'Where's my remote-controlled speedboat?' asked Trevor.

'Where's my case of Cuban cigars?' demanded Declan.

Padraic frowned. 'What are you guys doing here? I got a call saying that I'd won a prize, and that I was to collect it in Martin Moone's back garden.'

'Me too!' exclaimed Trevor. 'Although . . . it did seem like a *slightly* odd place to collect a prize.'

Declan's eyes narrowed. 'It's a set-up!

***BANOFFI PIE** – a pie made from bananas and toffee. Not to be confused with 'Tofana' pie, which is made from tofu and wrapped in a bandana.

Gentlemen, we've been duped,' he growled.

Padraic still seemed confused. 'So . . . do *you guys* have my banoffi pie?'

Declan spun around to see Martin standing behind them. 'Moone! You tricked us into coming here!'

'I'm sorry, I just . . . didn't think you'd show up otherwise. But I wanted to apologize.' He hung his head. 'I've been an ass. A big donkey's ass. I thought I was a genius, but I was a fool. A glory-hunting bossy pants. And I'm sorry.'

He looked at his friends. 'But I think we've come too far and tried too hard to give up now. Team Trepdem has got a place in tomorrow's Invention Convention. No one in our school has ever even been accepted before, so we're already history makers. And we've got the chance to make *even more* history. There's a half-built invention sitting right there in that workshop. An invention that can *win*. If we just give it one last push.'

'But Martin, there's not enough time,'

said Trevor. 'There's still tons of work to do, *and* we need to get it to Dublin by noon tomorrow.'

'That's the other side of the country!' exclaimed Padraic, showing off his geography skills.

'How ya gonna do that, Moone?' asked Declan.

'I can't do it,' admitted Martin. 'You can't do it either. None of us can. But I think *WE* can do it. If we work together.'

The three lads looked at each other.

Then finally Padraic gave a smile. 'Well, I *would* love to give that Tub Grub a test-drive . . .' He shrugged. 'What the heck. I'm in.'

'Me too,' agreed Trevor, with a grin.

Martin looked at Declan, who nodded. 'Let's get that gold.'

'Team Trepdem is back together!' cried Martin, punching the air.

'Yay!' cheered Padraic. 'Now where's that banoffi pie?'

*

The reunited team picked up right where they'd left off, but this time there was no boss and they figured out all the problems together. Martin realized that Padraic was right about the Taste Tanks – they needed to be spread out evenly or the tub would topple over. Trevor raided his mum's larder to fill the tanks, and Declan found a sturdier set of wheels to survive the cross-country trek to Dublin (borrowed from his mam's bicycle and his grandad's wheelchair).

They gave it everything they had, working all day and all night. They welded, glued, hammered, hummed, hawed, sawed, bashed, kicked, drilled, nailed, screamed, bled, bandaged, broke, cursed, fixed, argued, agreed, thought, consulted with their IFs, ignored their IFs, started a fire, fled, thanked Liam for putting out the fire, kicked Liam out again, got back to work, banged, scraped, cleaned, polished, stood back, marvelled, and at 6.48 in the morning . . . they were finished.

They wheeled it out of the workshop into the grey light of dawn and stared in disbelief at their creation. They had actually managed to build a mobile flavour bath. The Tub Grub 2000 was complete!

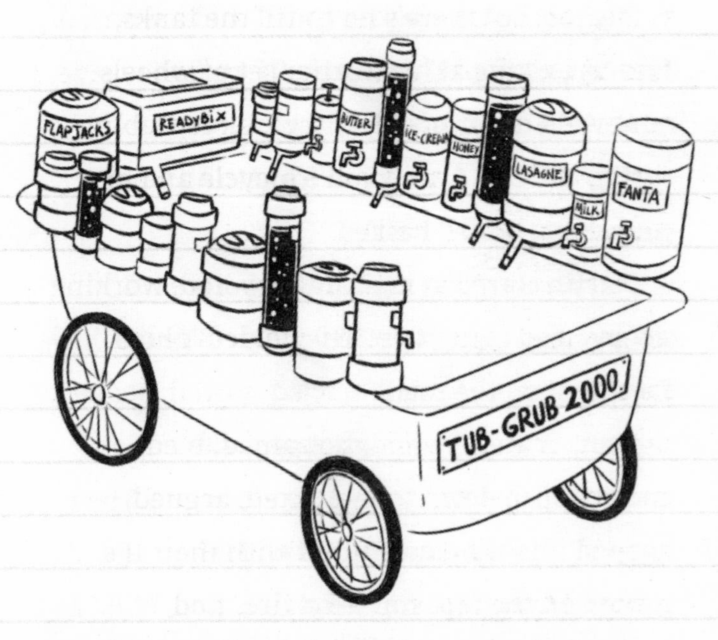

Declan brought over his motorbike, and Martin tied the bath to the back of it, using his signature knot – the Moone Mangle. And once

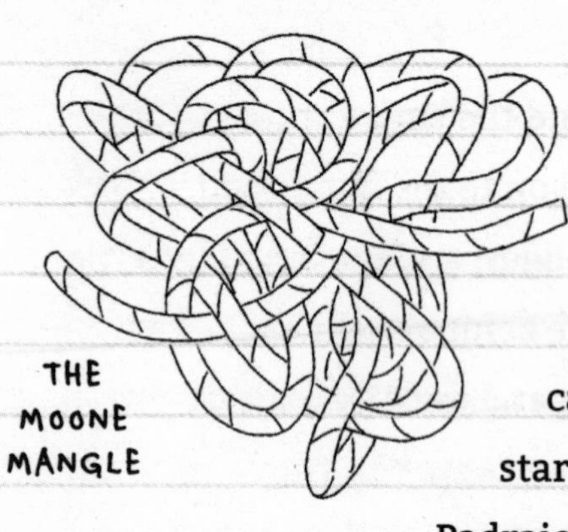

it was in place, they were ready to go.

'Hang on, we can't leave yet – I'm starving!' complained Padraic.

'Me too, but there's no time!' said a worried Trevor, looking at his watch. 'If we don't leave now, we'll never make it!'

'Eh, Martin? Aren't you forgetting what you've just built?' I asked.

Martin stared at me blankly before his sleepy head caught up. 'Of course! We can have breakfast on the road!'

Padraic and Trevor whooped with delight and stripped down to their underpants. They hopped into the fancy tub with Martin and turned on the taps for 'Readybix' and 'Milk' as Declan revved his motorbike and drove them down the driveway.

The engine roared, struggling to haul all

the extra weight, and the bath almost toppled over as they turned on to the main road. Milk splashed over the edges, and the boys clung on as they left Boyle behind and headed east towards the distant and dodgiest side of Ireland!

A sleepy Mammy Moone stared after them from her bedroom window. 'Where's Martin going in that weird bath?'

'No idea. But I'm changing the locks on my workshop before Declan gets back,' replied Liam, and scampered out of bed.

CHAPTER TWENTY-FOUR
BIRDMAGEDDON!

The boys were not very familiar with the Capital City. They'd heard rumours that breakfast didn't even exist there, so they were sure they'd made the right decision to immerse themselves in a giant breakfast bowl on the way. However, with a full bath, and three passengers swishing around in its Readybix stew, the Tub Grub 2000 was now extremely heavy. And Declan's motorbike was no Harley-Davidson*, so they struggled to reach the meagre speed of ten miles per hour. On stretches of downhill road, this would increase to around eighty miles

***HARLEY-DAVIDSON** – an iconic, powerful American motorcycle. Buyers are given a free tank of petrol, a patriotic bandana and a joke moustache with each purchase.

per hour, making the weighty cargo almost impossible to control.

As they crawled through the countryside, they got hoots and hollers from passers-by. Not always positive. Natives from the towns of Dromod, Mullingar and Rathowen wolf-whistled them. A trio of speed-walking grannies from Kinnegad made obscene hand gestures as they passed. And a labradoodle* from Longford mistook the bath for a porta-potty.

Their progress was horribly slow. Time was against them. And soon, something else was against them too – birds!

For several miles, flocks of the feathered fellas had been gathering overhead, making Padraic anxious.

'Why is that bunch of crows following us, Martin?'

***LABRADOODLE** – a breed of dog that has parents from the Labrador and Poodle families. This combination makes the dog very loyal, but too worried about ruining its hair to properly protect its owner.

'Murder!' Trevor blurted.

'What?! Why would they want to kill me?' Martin squealed.

'No, it's called a *murder* of crows, not a bunch.'

'Oh. Well, you can't just shout "murder!" like that. Not when I'm only wearing underpants.'

'Yeah, Trev,' Padraic agreed, 'that's the last thing we need, a fear of— Duck!'

'Ducks?' asked a confused Trevor. But when he saw Padraic and Martin quickly submerge themselves, he realized that 'Duck' was a command rather than a bird.

The crows were starting to attack, diving at the bath.

With their heads bobbing in and out of the water, the boys tried shooing them away with all their might.

'Shoo off! Shoo off, for flip sake, ya mad birds!' Padraic yelled. 'What do they flippin' want?'

'It's the Readybix!' Martin soon realized.

'They must know how delicious it is!'

'Eat faster!' urged Padraic, trying to force more of the sloppy cereal into his gob.

But the number of crows kept growing. There were hundreds of them. It was like a mass murder of crows. They dived at the bath, flapping and squawking, as they nabbed beakfuls of breakfast.

Other types of birds were joining the party too.

'Look! Seagulls!' I exclaimed, as I strolled alongside the bath.

'Maybe that means we're getting closer to dubby-Dublin!' cheered Loopy Lou, bounding along in his clown shoes.

'Or that every bird in the country has heard about the free Readybix,' added Crunchie.

On the motorbike, Declan was getting distracted by the feathered fracas. 'What the hell are ye doin' back there? It's not a flippin' bird bath I'm carrying!'

Martin yelled back to him, 'Give it everything

ya got, Declan! It's Birdmageddon back here!'

'Hold on, here we go . . .' said Padraic, who was holding a rock he'd snatched from the road. 'Don't fail me now . . . arm!'

He flung the rock desperately towards their aerial aggressors and – *Whack!* – he struck Declan square on the head.

'What ya do that for?!' Martin yelped.

'I was trying to hit two birds with one stone.'

The blow knocked Declan forward, and the motorbike swerved violently across the road. They narrowly avoided a telephone pole before veering into a roadside ditch.

Splosh!

The boys groaned in a daze, and Trevor clutched his leg where he'd received a small bruise. 'Well, at least now we know why they're called a "murder" of crows,' he muttered, as he pulled himself gingerly out of the tub.

The crash had scared off the birds for the moment, but the attack had left Team Trepdem with a new problem.

'Me bike!' Declan spluttered, as he shook his head clear.

They hauled the motorbike out of the dirty ditch and Declan pushed his foot repeatedly down on the starter pedal.

'She won't start,' he grumbled.

'Is the key in it?' asked Padraic unhelpfully.

'Yes, ya numpty, of course the key is in it. The engine is wrecked. Why wouldn't the key be in it?' barked Declan.

'I was just making conversation, to be honest. I feel like we don't have many conversations.'

Martin glanced at his watch, looking crestfallen. 'Well, lads, we've had a good run. But there's only half an hour left, and we've still got a long way to go. We'll never make it there on time now, but I think we've all learned some wise lessons for the future from this experience.'

'Like what?' Trevor spurted. 'When again in life will we need to know what not to put in a mobile bath to avoid an attack by birds?'

The boys slumped against the side of the tub – tired, defeated and dripping in milk.

'Our day will come, boys,' said Padraic cheerfully.

'Maybe it won't. How can you be sure we won't always just be a bunch of losers?' replied Trevor.

'Padraic's right,' said Martin. 'Every dog has his day. That's what my mam always says.'

Suddenly Declan sat up. He had a determined look in his eye, and a plan on his mind. He hopped to his feet, stuck his fingers between his lips, and blew a long, strange, piercing whistle that washed over the countryside like a wave.

'Me ears!' complained Trevor. 'Quit it, Mannion!'

'Every dog has his day!' Declan exclaimed. 'And this dog's day is today!'

He pulled out some rope from under the seat of his bike and grinned at them. 'We've got rope! Do we still have hope?'

'We're hopeless at hopelessness!' replied Martin defiantly.

'Then let's get this Grub-Tub to Dub!'

Moments later, the sound of dogs approaching filled the air – a sound they remembered very clearly from being chased around the Mannion home. Through the fields, the boys caught sight of an army of greyhounds galloping towards them.

Team Trepdem was back in action!

Soon, they were lashing the dogs to the front of the motorbike like skinny reindeer, and in no time they were road-ready. The boys bounded back into the bath, and Declan mounted his motorbike.

'Mush! My beautiful hounds, mush!!!' he called, imploring the dogs to move. And move they did. With incredible swiftness. In completely opposite directions!

'Hold! My stupid hounds, hold!!!'

The team looked worried.

'I guess they're used to *chasing* something,

not *carrying* something,' observed Padraic.

'Good idea, O'Dwyer!' Declan agreed, putting his fingers to his lips for another weird whistle.

'Was it?' Padraic asked. 'Yeah, it was, I suppose. I'm just the kind of lad who's never far from a great idea.'

In no time, Declan's horde of hares was racing towards them. The boys tied them to the front of the bike with longer ropes than they'd used on the greyhounds.

'Mush, me beautiful hares, mush!' yelled Declan. And finally they were off!

Martin, Padraic and Trevor clung to their

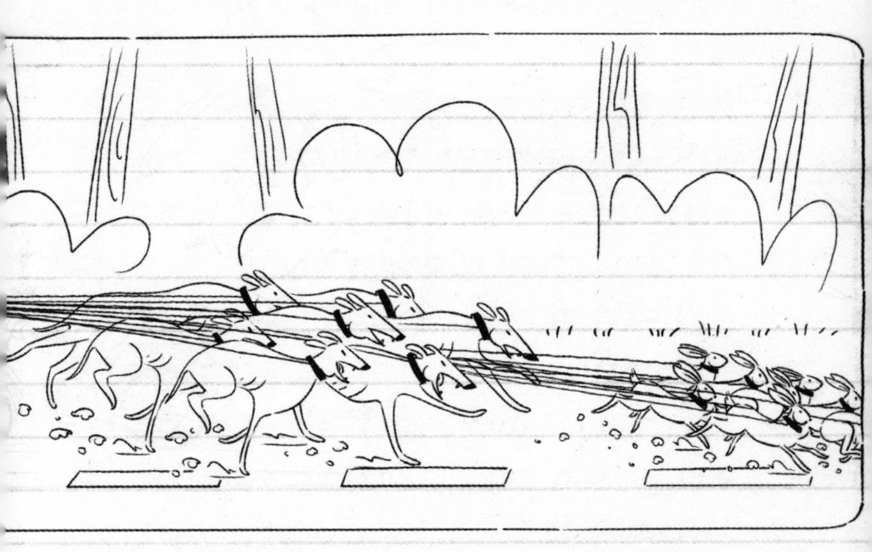

chariot, followed by birds, being hauled by the bike, that was pulled by the dogs, who were chasing the hares, who were running because they . . . just love the wind in their hair. It was a carrot-and-horse scenario*. But at immense speed. And there was a mobile flavour bath involved.

They hung on for dear life as they raced towards Dublin. They screeched around corners

*CARROT-AND-HORSE SCENARIO – holding a carrot in front of a horse, just out of reach, to make him go faster. It's the original version of an 'accelerator', and to reverse, you'd simply switch to broccoli.

with their tyres squealing and sparks flying as the bath grazed lamp posts and side-swiped post boxes. A couple of Taste Tanks got knocked off, but there was no time to stop.

'Four minutes left!' called Trevor, as they clattered through the city, causing cars to skid and swerve to avoid them. Dubliners stopped and stared at the sight, and Martin waved at them merrily.

'We're from the Countryside!' he yelled proudly.

They swerved around another corner, nearly capsizing once more – but finally the Convention Centre came into view.

'One minute to twelve!' called Trevor.

With a mighty bash, they mounted the kerb, and young scientists leaped left and right as they burst through the main doors of the Convention Centre, led by hares, greyhounds, followed by birds, and covered in milk – just as the clock struck noon.

CHAPTER TWENTY-FIVE
JUDGEMENT HOUR

'We made it!' cried Martin, punching the air, splashing milk at the crowd who had gathered around them.

'Greetings, fellow inventors!' called Padraic. 'We are Team Trepdem! Hear us roar!'

Padraic was the only one who roared this time, but several greyhounds starting howling too.

Security men arrived, looking befuddled, and informed them that pets were not permitted. They also suggested that the boys find some trousers.

The team hopped out, still hardly able to believe they'd got their invention to Dublin on time. But when they saw the state of the Tub Grub 2000, their happiness quickly faded.

It was a sorry sight indeed. The bath had taken quite a beating on the road. It was caked with dirt, dinged and dented, and completely splattered with bird poop.

'Oh balls . . .' I murmured, as one of the Taste Tanks tottered to the ground. Martin looked crestfallen, and I put a hand over his shoulder. 'Don't worry, buddy. I'm sure there'll be plenty of time to fix her up.'

But just then, an announcement came over the loudspeakers. 'Judging will now commence! Please have your inventions ready for inspection!'

The crowd dispersed as everyone ran back to their booths.

Martin was worried. 'How are we ever going to get this cleaned up in time for—'

But Declan was already arriving with a janitor's trolley full of cleaning supplies. He plucked a hammer and screwdriver from his bike and then unhitched the hares – 'Hup now. G'wan! Home with ye!!' – giving them a ten-second head start before untying the dogs who charged after them.

Martin located their booth, and the boys wheeled the bath over to it before getting down to work. They were so busy scrubbing and de-denting that they didn't even notice who was right next door to them.

'Well, if it isn't the Muckers,' came a mocking chuckle.

Martin looked up to see Vronny standing over him in her sunglasses. Beside her, the spiky-haired Max grinned out from his upturned collars.

'Well, if it isn't Lord and Lady Clean Boots,' replied Martin, rising to his feet.

'Easy, Martin,' whispered Padraic nervously.

'Hey, Hugh! Look what we found!' called Max.

'What is it, Maxo?'

Their teacher, Hugh, joined them with a swish of his perfumed hair. 'Ah, the boggers from Boyle! What are you doing out of Stench Land? Otherwise known as the *Country*.'

Max and Vronny sniggered, and Hugh fist-bumped them.

'What does it *look* like we're doing?' asked Martin.

'It looks like you're wiping bird poop off a weird-looking bath in your underpants,' observed Vronny.

'That's *exactly* what we're doing!' retorted Martin. 'But this isn't just a weird-looking bath.'

'It's also a weird-*smelling* bath,' added Max.

'It's a ground-breaking invention that is about to transform Planet Earth as we know it!' bragged Martin.

Hugh gave a snort. 'Well it's definitely transforming the carpet.'

He pointed to some strawberry jam that was leaking out of a Taste Tank.

'That's *meant* to be leaking!' insisted Martin.

'We should probably clean it up though, we don't want a stain,' murmured Padraic, and tossed a cloth to Martin.

'Still think you're gonna beat us?' scoffed Vronny.

Martin's eyes narrowed. 'Oh, we're gonna wipe the floor with you. Right after I wipe the floor with *this*!' he added, holding up the cloth.

Hugh gave another mocking chuckle. 'Look, kid, have you even seen my invention? I mean – *their* invention?'

He pointed to the booth next door where a gleaming silver robot stood to attention. It looked like a Garda – an Irish policeman – and was very impressive, although a bit scary too, holding a night stick* at its side.

'Power up, Garda Bot 10,000!' ordered Hugh.

The robot came to life at his command. It turned its head and spoke in an electronic voice. '*Hello, Master Hugh. Hello, civilians. Grand day, isn't it?*'

***NIGHT STICK** – a baton carried by police and riot squads. It's often called a 'billy club', after the more traditional way of dispersing riots, which was to release a herd of billy goats.

The boys were gobsmacked. 'It *is* a grand day,' murmured Padraic. 'How did it know that?'

'It knows everything,' bragged Hugh. 'It can give directions, stop crimes, and even detect lies!'

'Holy moly . . .' whispered Martin. 'It's incredible.'

'*Truth detected!*' confirmed the robot smugly.

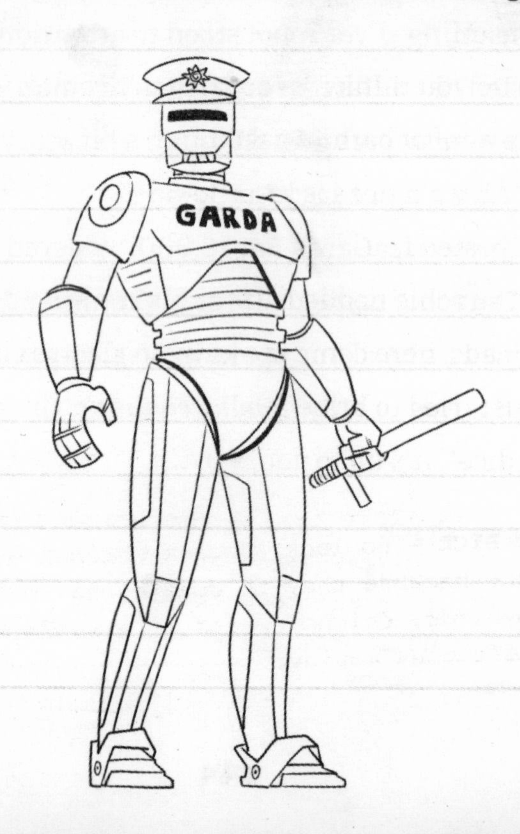

'You country bumpkins are way out of your depth,' sneered Hugh, 'so maybe you should just run back to your barns and hide under . . . whatever's in a barn.'

He turned and swaggered off with Max and Vronny.

Martin tried to hide it, but he was clearly quite intimidated by their impressive robot.

'How can we beat *that*?' he murmured to himself.

'Do you think it's too late to turn the bath into a *robot* bath?' I asked.

'All we'd need is some loopy-loopy-lightning!' suggested Lou.

Crunchie nodded. 'Or another electric fence!'

'Lads, here come the judges,' grunted Declan. 'I just tried to bribe them with a few cigars, but no dice*. It's up to you, Martin. Time to dance.'

***NO DICE** – no luck. Dice are considered lucky because they're covered in spots, like ladybirds, chimneysweeps or a rabbit's foot that's gone mouldy.

'You think I should dance?'

'Just . . . make them think it's brilliant. Dazzle them. And get that gold.'

Martin had absolutely no clue what he was going to say, but thankfully his trusty IF was right by his side.

'Don't worry, buddy – we've got this,' I assured him. 'Just don't hold back. *When in doubt, go all out*.'

The judges arrived, followed by a crowd of onlookers.

'Ah hello, Team Trepdem!' called a tall lady in the front with curly hair and bright, sparkling eyes. 'I'm Mrs Maggie Magoonty, founder of the Invention Convention, and these are my fellow judges,' she said, gesturing to some scientists beside her. 'We've been looking forward to this one. Your application sounded so exciting! *Science will not know what hit it* – right?'

'Eh. Right!' replied Martin uncertainly.

'Well then – let's see what hits it.'

Martin stepped to one side, revealing the

bath behind him. 'Behold! The thing that hits it!'

There was a pause. Not a pause of excitement and wonder, as Martin had hoped, but more like a pause of total bewilderment.

'What, eh . . . is it?' asked Mrs Magoonty blankly.

'Flip that question right back at her,' I advised.

'What . . . *isn't* it?' Martin asked her.

'A good invention!' shouted Max.

'Truth detected!' agreed the robot.

Hugh and Vronny laughed loudly, but Martin did his best to ignore them.

'Mrs Magoonty, let me answer your question with a question. How many times have you found yourself in the bath and cried out, *"I'd give anything right now for a flapjack"*?'

'Every Tuesday,' muttered Padraic.

'I don't think I've ever done that,' she answered.

'Well, no more!' shouted Martin. 'Because with this invention, *Suds Time* . . .' he said, holding up one hand, *'and Snack Time,'* he said, holding up his other hand, *'are now one.'* He linked his hands together dramatically. 'Ladies and gentlemen, I give you the Tub Grub—'

'20,000!' I whispered.

'The Tub Grub 20,000!' cried Martin.

'I thought it was 2000,' murmured Padraic.

'I just changed the name.'

'I love it. It's, like, ten times better!'

One of the scientists, a serious man with a moustache, frowned. 'So . . . this is a food delivery system . . . for a bath?'

'Now you're getting it, my friend,' replied Martin, who was strolling around now, growing in confidence, seeming to forget that he was wearing nothing but milk-covered underpants. 'But it's also so much more,' he went on. 'It's an all-you-can-eat bath buffet. It's a stadium snack stall. It's church chow. It's a party pool. It's where nibbling meets paddling. It's where you can take a dip *inside some dip*!'

His team-mates whooped at this, and there

was a round of applause from the crowd. But the judges seemed less convinced.

'Sorry, I'm confused,' said Mrs Magoonty. 'Isn't the purpose of a bath to get clean?'

'Isn't the purpose of a bath to feel good?' countered Martin.

'And you think that bathing in food would make you feel good?'

'Have you ever tried it?'

'I can't say I have.'

'Well now's your chance,' offered Martin, with a grin.

Mrs Magoonty smiled, and glanced at the other judges, but none seemed keen to hop into the bath.

'Maybe one of *you* could give us a demonstration,' she suggested.

'No problemo!' replied Martin, and turned to his pal. 'Padraic?'

Without a moment's hesitation, Padraic leaped into the tub, which was now clean after they'd scooped out all the Readybix. He lay down leisurely, and closed his eyes.

'Banoffi pie please, Martin!' he requested.

'We don't have banoffi pie,' whispered Martin.

'How about cheesecake?'

'Cheesecake fell off about fifty miles back,' muttered Trevor.

'Pancake syrup, did you say?' asked Martin loudly.

'Oh, eh, that might be a little hard to wash off,' worried Padraic.

But Martin had already turned on the tap. It oozed all over Padraic's belly.

'Oooohhh, lovely! That's the stuff. I'm hungry *and* need a wash, so I'm saving so much time here!'

'That's right, Padraic. And feel free to enjoy our accessories too.' Martin held them up, showing them to the crowd. 'A marshmallow sponge. Soup on a rope. And a rubber duck that *tastes like duck*!'

He handed this to the moustachioed scientist

who gave it a lick. 'Wow, it *really does* taste like duck!'

The crowd cheered again.

'Yeah! Give them the gold!' came a shout from behind the judges that sounded suspiciously like Declan Mannion.

Mrs Magoonty was applauding too. 'Well, it's certainly original, I'll give you that,' she told them. 'And every inventor worth their salt must be a true original. Well done, Team Trepdem. You didn't disappoint.'

She and the other judges wrote down numbers on their score-sheets and moved off. 'Right, who's next? Team Whimmion's?'

The robot sprang to life. '*Y'all ready for dis?*'

The gleaming Garda Bot started dancing to loud music, and the crowd followed the judges over to it, all craning to see, leaving Martin and his team alone again.

They looked at each other.

'Well – I guess that's that,' said Martin.

I winked at him proudly. 'Nice work, buddy.'

'Well done, Martin-meister, ya Moone-atic,' congratulated Padraic from the bath, gleaming with syrup.

'You too, P-Bucket,' replied Martin, with a grin. 'And you, T-Bird,' he said to Trevor. 'You too, Dectopolis.'

'Never call me that again,' warned Declan.

'Understood.'

'So what do we do now?' asked Trevor.

Martin shrugged. 'Now we wait.'

Padraic reclined in the bath and turned the syrup tap back on. 'Might as well get comfy,' he said, as he wallowed happily in the goo.

CHAPTER TWENTY-SIX
WINNERS

The team wheeled the bath, with Padraic inside it, to the far end of the hall, and were now standing among all the contestants, waiting for the judges to take to the stage. Tension was mounting, and the room was quiet, which was unfortunate because Padraic had swallowed too much syrup and was in the grips of a powerful sugar rush.

'*I'm the Candyman!*' he sang loudly.

'Hush!' hissed Martin.

'*The Candyman Man!*'

'Stop eating the syrup, Padraic!' whispered Martin. 'You're getting the sugar crazies*!'

***THE SUGAR CRAZIES** – a form of madness that sets in after your ninth lollipop where you can't decide if you want to dance, fight or puke, so end up doing all three at once.

'Yuppitty dee, Marty Magoo!' chirped Padraic, with a slippery salute.

The rest of the contestants started to applaud as the judges appeared, led by Mrs Magoonty.

'This is it, buddy,' I said with a grin. 'Don't forget to thank me in your winning speech!'

Martin gave a nervous smile. But no one looked as anxious as Trevor.

'I can't handle all this suspense,' he squeaked. 'Do you guys think we've won?'

Martin shrugged. 'Who knows? But no matter what, we've done well, Trev. *Amazingly* well. Just look at where we are.'

'A big room full of nerds,' observed Declan.

'A big room full of *winners*,' Martin corrected him. 'These are the best young inventors in Ireland. And we're right here with them. No matter what happens, no one can take that away from us.'

'You're right, Martin! I've never felt more like a winner in my whole life!' hollered Padraic.

His voice echoed around the hall and

everyone turned to stare at the underpants-wearing, syrup-slathered boy with a sugar-crazed smile.

'So, eh . . . as I was saying,' continued Mrs Magoonty, 'each invention was judged in four categories – originality, design, construction and usefulness. And the results are in.'

A tense silence descended over the hall.

'The winners of this year's Invention Convention are . . .'

I crossed my fingers, toes and ear lobes. 'Please, please, please,' I whispered.

'Team . . . Whimmion's!'

My heart sank, my ear lobes sagged, and my whole body slumped with disappointment.

Martin and his team-mates were quiet, but they clapped politely, heroically, along with everyone else. They watched Max, Vronny and Hugh bound on to the stage, followed by their impressive Garda Bot, who slowly mounted the steps.

'Boom!' shouted Hugh into the mic. 'Victory is ours!'

'Yes! In your face, losers!' yelled Max.

'Aww, look at all those sad faces out there. Sorry not sorry,' sneered Vronny.

'Congratulations, Team Whimmion's,' said Mrs Magoonty, looking annoyed by their bragging as she handed over the trophy and gold medals.

'Thanks, Big Maggie, thanks a lot!' said Hugh. He returned to the mic. 'Ya know, just being a part of this Invention Convention thingy is a real honour. But you know what's an even greater honour? Beating every one of you!'

He paused for laughter, but the room remained silent.

'Seriously though, it means so much to me. And the robot. And to them,' he added, pointing at Max and Vronny, 'the kids who built the robot.'

'*Lie detected!*' blurted the Garda Bot.

'What?'

Hugh glanced at the robot, then chuckled.

'Ha! He's just . . . overexcited.'

'Lie detected!'

Hugh tried to ignore it, pressing on with his speech. 'Ya know, when Vronzer and Maxo came up with this robot idea and asked for my advice on construction—'

'Lie detected! My chief engineer was Vladimir Petrovski—'

'Shut that thing up, Maxo!' snapped Hugh.

'What did it say?' asked Mrs Magoonty, stepping forward.

'Nothing! It's just malfunctioning. Power down, Garda Bot!' he ordered.

'Do NOT power down!' she interjected.

'Conflicting orders! Confusion!'

Mrs Magoonty strode forward and took command. 'Garda Bot, are you malfunctioning?'

'Power down!' hissed Hugh.

'Not *another word* from Team Whimmion's,' warned Mrs Magoonty.

The robot beeped. '*All systems functioning perfectly.*'

'Then answer me this, Garda Bot. Where were you built?' she asked.

'In an underground lab in Russia.'

There was a gasp around the room and Mrs Magoonty's expression hardened.

'By whom?'

'By a team of robotic scientists who then secretly shipped me to a school called St Whimmion's – which, I was informed, is the greatest school ever and all other schools are a bunch of losers.'

Mrs Magoonty turned to face the Whimmion's trio, who stood there sheepishly, clutching their trophy and medals.

'Well, it might be the greatest school ever, but it's *YOU* who are the losers today,' she informed them angrily. 'The rules state that all inventions must be built by students alone. So you are hereby disqualified for cheating.'

The room erupted with a loud cheer.

Mrs Magoonty glared at Hugh. 'And as their

teacher, you will pay the ten-thousand-pound fine and serve a short but unpleasant sentence in jail.'

'What?!'

'It was stated very clearly on the entry form. Now please hand back your trophy and medals, and you'll be escorted from the stage.'

Security men started to approach from either side.

'No! You can't do this! We're the winners!' insisted Hugh. But the security men kept coming closer. 'C'mon, Maxo and Vronzer – RUN!'

He snatched the night stick from the Garda Bot and leaped into the crowd, clutching the trophy.

'Arghhhhhh!' came the screams, as young inventors fled left and right.

Amid the chaos, Hugh, Max and Vronny made for the exit.

'Catch them, nerds!' ordered Declan from across the hall.

'They're getting away!' fretted Loopy Lou. 'We gotty-gots to do something, Trevvy!'

'Wake up!' Crunchie yelled at Padraic, who'd nodded off in the bath.

'Hmmm?'

I turned to Martin. 'I've got an idea, buddy. How good is your aim?'

'Weak and wobbly,' he answered honestly.

'Well it'll have to do. Launch him, Martin!'

'Launch him?!' exclaimed Crunchie and Lou.

Martin seized the side of the tub.

'Help him, Trevvy!' called Lou, and Trevor gripped the other side. Declan realized what they were up to and grabbed the back.

'Roll like the wind, Padraic,' whispered Martin.

'Huh?'

And with that, the three amigos gave the Tub Grub an almighty shove. It zoomed away with a confused Padraic inside it, who was thankfully too sugared-up to be frightened. He sped across the room, miraculously missing several students, and was making a beeline for the fleeing fraudsters. The bath was on a direct course to intercept them!

But unfortunately, as often happens in life, there was a bin in the way.

BOOM!

The bath smashed into it and vaulted Padraic into the air.

'Wooooooh!' he squealed. 'I'm flying!'

Like a wingless, greasy angel, he soared majestically over the heads of the stunned students, dripping syrup from his slippery stomach.

'I feel like a swan!' he called, waving cheerfully at the upturned faces.

But as every young scientist knows, gravity has a way of asserting itself, and what goes up – even if it thinks it's a swan – usually comes back down.

SPLAT!

Padraic landed perfectly on top of Hugh, who

crumpled to the ground as Max and Vronny fell headlong over them. All four tumbled across the floor and collapsed in a heap.

The security men were upon them in seconds, and Mrs Magoonty swiftly reclaimed the trophy and medals.

'You and your cheating school are banned forever!' she declared, and the security men hauled them off.

'Told ya we'd beat you!' Martin yelled after them.

And indeed they had.

'The trophy will now go to the runners-up!' announced Mrs Magoonty.

Martin suddenly turned to his team-mates. 'Wait – if they're eliminated . . . does that now mean that *we've won?!!!'*

They all looked at each other, with their hearts in their mouths. Could this really be true? Did this twist of fate mean that Team Trepdem had now come first?!!

Well, dear reader old pal, I'm sorry to say that

the answer was no. Team Trepdem had received top marks for originality, but hadn't quite aced the other categories. They would have won if they'd been in second place, but they were in twelfth place, so moved triumphantly up to eleventh – which, out of a hundred inventions, wasn't half bad!

Every team was presented with a certificate, which had the word 'Participant' printed proudly across it, to the delight of the gang. Declan was particularly pleased that it was written in gold lettering (which he would later try to melt down and accidentally set on fire).

And for bravely apprehending the villains, Padraic received an extra gift – a banoffi pie.

'We're no losers! We're *Participants*! We take part! We're take-parters!' declared Martin happily, as they posed for their official team photo.

*

The promised dance party kicked off and soon the place was awash with tea and buns. Padraic passed out on the floor, and while the boys drew a moustache on him, I wandered off among the exhibits.

I soon discovered that this Invention Convention wasn't just for Realsies, and in the same way that the Museum of Tractors had imaginary exhibits, this place had imaginary inventions too. I heard applause in the distance and followed it to a room where a crowd of imaginaries were congratulating the competition winner. He was wearing a strange contraption, and I smiled when I saw his familiar face.

'Wilbert!' I exclaimed, and he hopped towards me happily, carrying a trophy. 'You won?!'

'It seems so!' he chuckled. 'I kept working on that Wonkey Self-Milker that I invented on our way home from the quest, and it proved to be quite the hit!'

With his hoof, he pressed a button on the contraption on his belly and some green milk squirted out. It was impressive – but I also felt a twinge of guilt.

'Wilbert, I'm sorry I wasn't better at milking you and looking after you. I wanted to be the best pet owner ever . . . but I let you down. Maybe I'm just not cut out for it.'

Wilbert frowned, confused. 'But Sean – I owe all of this to you! When you brought me on the quest for the Notion Potion, you changed my life! Without you, I'd still be eating rocks and trying to swallow my own elbows – instead of contributing to science and improving the lives of imaginaries everywhere!' He lay a hoof on my shoulder. 'I thank the day that Martin gave me to you, Sean – the finest IF that a Wonkey could ever wish for.'

He gave me a hug and then bounded away, leaving me with a tear in my eye and his weird milk on my shirt.

'Well, at least the Notion Potion helped *someone*,' noted Crunchie, joining me with a grin.

'So our questeroo wasn't a big failure after all!' added Loopy Lou brightly. 'Even if it didn't help your Realsie.'

'Actually, I think it *did* help him,' I mused. 'When Martin thought he'd drunk the Notion Potion, he let his imagination run wild. He got crazy-creative, and unleashed an idea that beat some of the smartest kids in the country. His imagination *unlocked* his imagination, which, when you think about it, is some mind-bending science!'

'No, Sean – *that's* some mind-bending science!' blurted Loopy Lou, and raced off towards an imaginary invention – a mini tornado that was shooting gumdrops in every direction. 'I gotta gets me one of those!'

'Wait for me!' called Crunchie, hurrying after him.

I was about to follow when I noticed another exhibit nearby. It showed a picture of Barney Bunton, imaginary friend to the inventor Harry Ferguson, and I wandered over to it.

The exhibit gave some history about the pair, and I discovered that Barney was a bit of a mad genius, just like his Realsie, and had a few odd quirks. For example, he liked to play the violin to birds, he washed his feet in a basin of unicorn spit every morning, and he had a weird habit of collecting his nose pickings in a small bottle.

I paused when I read this last titbit.

Nose pickings . . .

I pulled out the little bottle that I'd borrowed from Barney's hat and read the label again.

N.P.

No way. It *couldn't* be. Could it . . . ?

If it was, then Harry and Barney had nothing to do with Notion Potion at all. Which also meant that the Mad Mechanic really *did* think of all those incredible inventions himself.

I shook the bottle, peering inside it.

And it also meant that those nasty, shrivelled-up, crunchy things that I'd eaten were in fact . . .

Oh balls.

CHAPTER TWENTY-SEVEN
EOPS

The gang returned home to Boyle, and life got back to normal. Things had changed a lot since Martin had embarked on this crazy adventure. He was no longer sharing a house with a trio of triumphant sisters, but they, like Martin, had realized that winning was overrated. And in some ways, they'd all managed to win anyway.

Having lost her sack-punching battles, Sinead had decided to start *growing* potatoes instead of smashing them, and soon she was happily tending to a flurry of little green shoots in the back garden. It was the first time she'd ever tried to create something rather than destroy it, and although she'd have an occasional slip-up, where she'd suddenly stomp or punch one of them, most of the time she took pretty good care of those spudlings, to the astonishment of the other Moones.

Fidelma had abandoned her goal of becoming the first female Taoiseach of Ireland (for the moment at least), but had no regrets, as she was madly in love for the first time in her life. And although nobody could really understand what she saw in the dorky Dessie Dolan, there was no denying that she was positively *glowing* these days.

Things also took an unexpected turn for Trisha. Her junk-jewellery business had been going well, but it turned out that she'd never bothered to clean her recycled rubbish, so a lot of her customers got infections. Her trash trinkets also began to stink, and hungry cats followed poor Linda around until she finally tossed out her tuna-can earrings. But the Power-Power Ties were the worst disaster. They began leaking battery acid, which burned through expensive shirts and left a nasty rash on the skin. The town mayor was covered in blotches and was threatening to sue.

But Trisha didn't seem in the least bit bothered. In fact, she was quite tickled by all the trouble she'd created, and pretended that she'd planned it all out, bragging that she'd pulled off the greatest 'fake fashion scam' in the history of Boyle.

So in the end, none of them did what they set out to do, but what they did, in some ways, made them a lot happier.

'Maybe you're right, Sean,' said Martin, as we sat on the back wall pondering all this. 'Maybe you *can* win without winning. I wanted to get my face on the Winners Wall, and even though I didn't quite get there, I sure as flip don't feel like a loser. I guess what matters most is to be . . . *a Participant*!'

He ripped open his shirt to reveal his Participant certificate, which he was wearing on a chain around his neck.

I sighed. 'Martin, do you have to rip open your shirt *every time* you say the word "Participant"?'

'I do, Sean, yes,' he admitted, 'I'm afraid I do.'

*

As Martin entered his final week of primary school, he was still keen to leave his mark in some way, and brainstormed ideas with Padraic about what to do on their last day.

'I'm gonna be Martin Mayhem!' he proclaimed. 'We've gotta do the maddest stuff, the craziest things we can think of – so no one forgets that Marty Moone and Padraic O'Dwyer walked these halls!'

Padraic nodded excitedly. 'I know what'll make everyone remember me. I'll knit them all lovely scarves!'

'What? No! I'm talking about doing *destructive* stuff.'

'OK, how about this? Let's turn all the globes into snow globes!'

'Let's turn *him* into a snow globe,' I muttered.

'How about *this*?' said Martin. 'Let's use the toilet all day and not flush it. And then blow it up!'

'That's more like it!' I cried.

'Let's steal all the chalk and hide it,' giggled Padraic, 'but then, in a twist, tell them where it is!'

'That's *less* like it.' I sighed.

They continued to concoct ideas, but as they strolled to school on their last day, the pair were still no closer to a plan.

'Let's turn all the chairs back to front,' proposed Padraic, 'but sit back to front on them, so we're facing the right way!'

'Let's put the chairs on the tables, and the tables on the chairs,' suggested Martin. 'And then blow them up!'

'Let's shave naughty words into our beards!' blurted Padraic.

'We don't have beards,' Martin reminded him.

'Let's grow beards!'

'Yeah! Actually . . . we might not have time for that, seeing as it's now our last day of school,' noted Martin as they came to a stop outside the old drab building.

'Look! They put up a sign!' marvelled Padraic.

It was hanging on the front of the school and read: 'Goodbye, Sixth Class. We'll Miss You'.

'I gotta get in there!' squealed Padraic, and he ran off, kicking over a bin with excitement.

'This is it, buddy. Time for some mayhem!' I cried.

But as Martin stared at the sign, his eyes started brimming with tears, and his voice cracked as he murmured quietly, 'I don't want to leave.'

Instead of trashing his school that day, like most of his other classmates were doing, Martin wandered around delivering long, heartfelt goodbyes to everyone and every *thing* that he encountered.

'Bye-bye, blackboard. Bye-bye, chairs. Bye-bye, broken projector – I'm going to miss *you* most of all,' he said fondly.

He gave a long hug to a confused Trevor in the corridor, and he found Declan Mannion in the yard, sliding a heavy manhole-cover back into place.

'Need a hand, Dec?' he offered.

'Nah, all done, Moone,' replied Declan. 'I just squeezed Principal Maloney's favourite chair into the sewer. He won't be finding that in a hurry!'

'Oh Declan, you old scamp,' Martin chuckled affectionately.

'Huh?'

'It's been an honour primary-schooling with you.'

'Eh. Yeah. Have fun in your stupid new school, Moone.'

Martin frowned. 'Aren't you going to be there too?'

'Nah. Jermaine is holding me back for another year. Says I failed everything – even science! Can you believe that sack of nonsense?' asked Declan with a smirk. 'Maybe he's right – maybe we *will* be spending the rest of our lives together in that flippin' classroom! Anyway, I better run. I'm gonna try to flip over his car. Later, Moone!'

He swaggered off, still wearing Liam's jacket, and bouncing his old handball.

'They're holding him back *again*?!' I asked in disbelief.

'Not if I can help it,' said Martin with a determined frown. 'Ya know, Sean, there's a reason that the Team Trepdem slogan is *No man left behind!*'

'I thought your slogan was *Rub-a dub-dub, let's build a Tub Grub!*'

'Oh yes, that's it!' he replied. 'What a great slogan! Rub-a dub-dub, let's build a Tub Grub!' he proclaimed, and then marched into the school.

Moments later, he was back in his old classroom confronting his teacher.

'You can't hold Declan back another year. He deserves to graduate with the rest of us!' implored Martin.

Mr Jackson was clutching a hurley stick* and kept glancing out the window nervously. 'Moone, in case you hadn't noticed, we're a little

***HURLEY STICK** – a stick for playing the Irish game of hurling, which is a mixture of running, fighting and Kendo (the ancient art of wooden swordplay). A little ball is involved too – so there's also a touch of golf.

busy here. All hell is breaking loose outside, and Principal Maloney has lost something very dear to him.'

The worried-looking principal was searching the classroom behind Martin. 'It's a newly upholstered, leather swivel-chair. I popped out to the bathroom, and then it was gone! How can it have just vanished?!' he asked, bewildered.

Martin turned back to his teacher. 'You said that Declan failed science – but that was probably because he was spending so much time on our science project!'

'What science project?'

'For the Invention Convention!'

'Don't talk nonsense, Moone!' snapped Mr Jackson as the Bonner brothers raced past the window, wearing traffic cones on their heads.

'Jermaine, you never mentioned that your students took part in the *Invention Convention*,' said the impressed principal.

'Ehh . . .'

Mr Jackson turned to Martin blankly. 'Did they?'

'We didn't just take part, sir. We were *Participants*!' the boy declared, ripping open his shirt.

Unfortunately, Martin had forgotten to wear his 'certificate chain' that day, so his dramatic shirt-ripping simply exposed his bare belly, which was both confusing and disturbing.

'Whoa, whoa, keep your shirt on, Moone,' beseeched his disgusted teacher.

'I'm confused,' said the principal, 'and not just by the shirt thing. Are you saying that *Declan Mannion* was involved in this too? *The* Declan Mannion?'

'The one and only, sir,' confirmed Martin.

'Did you *force* him to do this? Blackmail him somehow?'

'He forced *us*!' retorted Martin. 'Wouldn't take no for an answer. He's science-mad, that fella. And gold-mad.'

The principal was still trying to wrap his

head around all this. 'So Declan *voluntarily* took part in an *extra-curricular science activity*?'

'We couldn't have done it without him!' exclaimed Martin. 'He held team meetings in his house, invested his own cash in the project, forged—'

'Maybe don't mention that part, buddy,' I interjected.

'Eh . . . Loaned us his own bath,' continued Martin, 'and used his dogs and hares to pull us all the way to Dublin!'

Mr Jackson and Principal Maloney were so baffled that Martin had to recount the entire story of their adventure, but it wasn't until he whipped out the team photograph that they finally started to believe him.

Just then, Declan ambled past the classroom door, carrying a car wheel under his arm.

'Declan!' yelled the principal.

Declan poked his head into the room and nodded to them. 'Mr M, Jermaine, Moone face.'

Principal Maloney grilled him about

everything that Martin had told them, and asked if it was true.

Declan hung his head.

'Yeah I did it,' he confessed. 'I did it all. Was it for the gold? Maybe. Was it just to stop my dad enjoying his nightly baths? Possibly. Or was it just to get Liam Moone's lovely coat? Probably. But whatever the reason, I became a dork for a while. I did science stuff out of school and hung with some eejits who all talk to invisible people. No offence, Martin. And Martin's imaginary friend.'

'None taken,' we both replied.

Principal Maloney gave a broad smile.

'Well, Declan, if you're the sort of student who can work with a team to build a mobile flavour bath, transport it to Dublin with a pack of greyhounds and hares, while fending off a flock of hungry birds, and then take part in the biggest science competition in the country, then you're certainly ready for secondary school.'

Declan looked stunned as the principal shook

his hand. 'Congratulations, Mr Mannion. Today is your last day.'

'EOPS!' Martin whooped with glee, punching the air.

Mr Jackson smirked. 'Looks like we're finally getting divorced, Declan.'

'About time, Jermaine. Here's a break-up present,' he said, handing him the tyre.

'What do I need this for?' asked a confused Mr Jackson.

'To go home,' Declan said bluntly. 'C'mon, Moone. Let's roll.'

They turned to go.

'Declan, one last thing,' started the principal. 'I don't suppose you've seen my—'

Declan tossed him a crowbar. 'You'll need this to find it, Mr M. Just follow your nose.'

And with that, he and Martin strolled out of their classroom for the very last time.

CHAPTER TWENTY-EIGHT
GRADUATION

Martin and Declan walked down the corridor while the sounds of chaos and destruction emanated from the yard outside. Declan was quiet, and still seemed a bit stunned.

'I'm not sure what you did back there,' he said, 'but you seem to have got me out of this place.'

Martin shrugged. 'Think nothing of it, Mr Mannion.'

'Listen, Moone, I've never thanked anyone for anything before.'

Martin smiled, waiting to soak up some sweet, sweet gratitude.

'And I'm not about to start now,' continued Declan.

Martin's smile disappeared. 'Understood.'

'But you've done me a favour, Moone. And some day I shall repay that favour. When you least expect it . . . ' he warned.

Martin gave a confused nod, unsure if he was being thanked or threatened. 'OK. I'll . . . look forward to it?' he replied uncertainly.

They walked on.

'Ya know, Moone, normally I fly solo, so this team thing was kinda weird for me. But it was also . . . kinda fun. Maybe we should all get together again sometime. And do something less nerdy. Like rob a bank or something,' suggested Declan.

Martin gave a thoughtful nod. 'Maybe . . .'

Declan stopped at a door that led outside. 'Well, I better go. I started a fire out there and I should really keep an eye on it.'

'Good thinking. Ya wouldn't want it to blow out.'

Declan took off Liam's jacket and tossed him the handball. 'I think these belong to your old man,' he said, and then strolled outside.

'Keep it real, Moone face!'

'Actually I prefer to keep it imaginary!' chirped Martin.

Declan gave a confused glance back, and then wandered off.

The door slammed shut, and we were on our own again.

I looked to Martin, proud of the little eejit. 'Well, you wanted to do something big before you left, and I think you might have just done it, buddy. Your invention adventure just got Declan Mannion graduated. And this school will never be the same without him.'

Martin grinned. 'Not quite as good as a blown-up toilet, but not bad, I suppose.'

We turned and then noticed where we were standing – right back where this had all started.

'Bye-bye, Winners Wall,' murmured Martin, as he gazed at the shiny trophies and framed photographs of triumphant teams.

I looked to the corner above it. 'The mould has grown. Your chin's gotten a lot bigger.'

'Well, if that's the only version of Martin Moone that's going to be up on that wall, then that's fine by me. I couldn't give two hoots about winning any more,' he declared.

I nodded, and we both continued to stare at the wall.

'Still, though . . . it *would* be nice to be up there,' I said wistfully.

He turned to me, with a mischievous look in his eye. 'Are you thinkin' what I'm thinkin'?'

'Always!'

Martin glanced around, whipped out the photo again, and wedged it into one of the picture frames, covering up some old football team.

He gazed proudly at the snap of Team Trepdem.

'That's more like it,' he said with a grin.

*

We strolled outside and found ourselves walking through utter chaos. Declan was stoking a fire where a gang of sixth-classers were burning their school uniforms. Several younger kids were kicking Mr Jackson's car, which had been flipped on to its side and spray-painted with the words 'Drive this!'

Trevor charged past us, pushing Loopy Lou

in a wheelbarrow and blaring rap music from a boom box. Principal Maloney was trying to prise open the manhole, and Mr Jackson was charging after students with his hurley stick. He spotted the Bonner brothers trying to graffiti the word 'graffiti' on the wall, but they'd completely misspelled it.

'Ya stupid fools. That isn't how ya spell "graffiti"!' he roared, and chased them away.

At the far side of the yard, Martin turned to look back at the drab old building where he'd spent so much of his young life.

'Bye-bye, school,' he mumbled softly.

Padraic charged past us, waving the Roscommon flag. He'd clearly embraced his destructive side at last, as he'd burned his uniform and was back in his underpants.

'We've done it, Martin! We've taken over the asylum!' he screamed with glee.

'Viva la Revolution!' cheered Crunchie Haystacks, who cartwheeled behind him.

I laughed and led Martin away. 'Come on, Mayhem. Let's get you home.'

'Ya know what I might have tonight?' he asked as we ambled out through the school gates.

'A lovely bath?' I guessed.

'Bingo! But I'm also a bit peckish,' he added. 'Do we still have that chicken soup Taste Tank?'

'No, I think that one fell off on the way home,' I told him. 'But peanut butter is still fully stocked.'

'A bath of peanut butter,' he pondered thoughtfully. 'Yes, that'll do, Sean,' said the Moone boy. 'That'll do me nicely.'

THE END

ACKNOWLEDGEMENTS

Special thanks to:

Our editors Lucy Pearse and Venetia Gosling for all the cajoling, howls of encouragement, forceps and suction cups that helped us birth this book from our conjoined womb.

Our incredible illustrator, Walter Giampaglia of Cartoon Saloon, for filling these pages with his brilliant drawings that look *exactly* like they were done by a talentless twelve year old.

Our agent Robert Kirby for demanding that we get paid in crisps.

And to Nick's brother-in-law, Brian Goodman, for helping us do the first sketches of Wilbert, based on his own close encounter with a Wonkey behind a wheelie bin.

Research on Harry Ferguson was done with the help of a fantastically detailed biography called *Harry Ferguson: Inventor and Pioneer* by Colin Fraser (Old Pond Publishing). If you want to find out more about him, his famous 'Black Tractor' can be found in the Science Museum, London. You can also visit the Ferguson Family Museum on the Isle of Wight.

The Invention Convention was inspired by the BT Young Scientist and Technology Exhibition held in Dublin every year. To find out more, visit: www.btyoungscientist.com

If you're in the UK, there's the annual Big Bang UK Young Scientists and Engineers Competition. More information at www.thebigbangfair.co.uk

Or find your own science competition wherever you live. Invent, imagine, and if you explode anything, blame it on your IF.

About Chris O'Dowd

Chris O'Dowd is an award-winning actor and writer from the barmy town of Boyle in Ireland. Chris did some good acting in *Bridesmaids*, *The IT Crowd*, *Gulliver's Travels*, *Of Mice and Men* and *The Incredible Jessica James*. We won't mention the films where he did bad acting. He has a dog called Potato and a cat who shouts at him for no reason. He studied at University College Dublin and the London Academy of Music and Dramatic Art. He graduated from neither. Chris created *Moone Boy* to get revenge on his sisters for putting make-up on him as a child. He co-wrote the Sky TV series and the Moone Boy books with his good friend Nick Murphy, who is a lot older than Chris.

ABOUT NICK V. MURPHY

Nick V. Murphy is a writer from Kilkenny, Ireland. (The V. in his name stands for Very.) He went to Trinity College Dublin to study English and History, but spent most of his time doing theatre and running away from girls. This was where he bumped into Chris O'Dowd, who was out looking for pizza. After college, Nick focused on writing, which was the laziest career he could think of, as it could even be done while wearing pyjamas. He wrote a few things for TV, then a movie called *Hideaways*, before co-writing a short film with Chris called *Capturing Santa*. The pyjama-wearing pair developed this into the comedy series *Moone Boy*, which has won an International Emmy for Best Comedy.

MORE MARVELLOUS MOONE BOY BOOKS!

'Hilarious and brilliant'
Frank Cottrell-Boyce

'Raucously funny'
Irish Times

Short stories, a comic strip, activities and games!